Easter Lilies

An Appalachia-Inspired Short Story Collection

The Broken Petals Short Stories Series

Jan-Carol
Publishing, Inc

"every story needs a book"

Easter Lilies
An Appalachia-Inspired Short Story Collection
The Broken Petals Short Stories Series

Published April 2017
Mountain Girl Press
Imprint of Jan-Carol Publishing, Inc

ISBN: 978-1-945619-22-9

You may contact the publisher:
Jan-Carol Publishing, Inc
PO Box 701
Johnson City, TN 37605
publisher@jancarolpublishing.com
jancarolpublishing.com

This is dedicated to all the talented authors for their participation in this delightful collection of short stories, and to all the readers of Jan-Carol Publishing's books.

Table of Contents

Easter Lilies

High Time: Get a Load of Those Shoes

Rebecca Spindler

Earlene strode out of the choir room and headed for the coat rack. Her cherry red patent leather pumps turned heads. "Oh, these!" Earlene smiled. "I haven't worn these shoes since Joey and Lisa's wedding. I'm breaking them back in before my trip to Bermuda."

"See! I told you, she's fixin' to leave Clyde," quipped Mona Jean to Luann. Luann and the other choir members' eyes all widened with surprise. It didn't take much to stir the gossip pot at Our Holy Redeemer church, especially among the choir members, who assembled every Tuesday night. If only they had used their sweetly-tuned voices for the intended greater good.

"You'd just love that, wouldn't you?! Well, here's a newsflash: I'm not leaving my husband. I'm just...leaving the country."

"What for?" Luann asked meekly. "Is everything all right at home, Earlene?" butted in Pastor Rutledge. Earlene looked as though she might blow a gasket. She stepped out of her pumps and tossed them in a Publix tote bag, then she pulled on her thick winter boots and marched towards the door. As she swung the heavy church doors wide open, a blast of frigid January air burst in. The choir members shuddered. Earlene, defiant and determined, turned to them as she fastened her long wool coat and adjusted her hand-knitted cap.

"Everything is wine and roses at home, Reverend. I am fine, and Clyde is fine. I just figure it's high time I take some 'me' time while there's still a 'me' left." And with that, Earlene strutted out into the winter's night with the wind at her back.

The old Chevy SUV sputtered to life, and Earlene put it into gear as the snow drifts swirled across Route 58. The curvy road leading out of town in these conditions would've been treacherous to most drivers, but not to Earlene. She had lived in these hilly parts of Virginia her entire life. Her daddy taught her at an early age how to maneuver a vehicle down these narrow roads and hairpin turns. She loved the challenge and beauty of snow. But this winter, she'd had enough: enough snow, enough silence. Enough sorrow.

Just three months prior, Earlene had laid her mother to rest. Now she was an orphan. Granted, she had been blessed with 67 years of a healthy existence. She didn't know how long it would be before illness and fragility showed up on her doorstep, but she wasn't about to wait around to find out. On a whim, she had taken a detour from her weekly grocery shopping trip and stopped by a travel agency in Bristol. After an hour, she had bought herself a cruise to Bermuda. Lucky for her, she and the church choir had travelled to Niagara Falls the previous summer, to perform at a very dignified international church event. Her passport was just begging to be put to use again. That ticket would be a huge upheaval to Earlene's mundane existence.

At home, her husband Clyde plopped himself down in his recliner, his baggy eyes glued to Fox News. She swore he had a thing for that blond bombshell, Megyn Kelly. Harmless as his infatuation was, Earlene had become accustomed to Clyde tuning her out. And she did the same to him. They co-existed, cordially. Clyde was five years her senior, and was a man very set in his ways. The man lived by routine: a routine Earlene had created, or rather, established to perfection. Coffee at 6 AM. Biscuits, butter, and jelly by 6:20 AM, and it *has* to be strawberry jelly. Earlene substituted with raspberry once, and she never heard the end of Clyde's complaints about tiny raspberry seeds disrupting his dentures. Newspaper at 6:30 AM, and *Fox News* at 7 AM.

When the TV came on, Earlene went out. On Mondays, she played cards with Edna, a childhood friend in assisted living. "Are you sure you want to do this? Bermuda is just a tiny island. What if a hurricane comes and washes you away?" Edna warned. Tuesday was casserole day, and choir practice after supper. Wednesday meant a trip to the library and book club over lunch. "Make sure you know where to find the lifeboats," recommended Myrna, the librarian, as she handed Earlene the latest edition of *British Isle Vacations*. "You just never know what will happen out at sea." Thursdays, Earlene volunteered at the humane society, cuddling with kittens and cleaning out litter boxes. "My cousin went on one of them big cruise ships. Some kind of virus went rampant, and he ended up in his cabin the whole time, barfing his brains out," laughed Brandon, the college kid who exercised the big dogs. All this unsolicited advice made Earlene's head swim. Through it all, she just smiled, held her tongue and bided her time. Friday was errands day" driving to the post office, paying bills at the bank, and picking up more groceries. No TGIF for Earlene. Since she and Clyde were both retired, the only thing they had to thank God for was the ability to live and breathe each day and prepare to repeat the routine for the upcoming week.

On the occasional Saturday, their son and daughter-in-law would bless them with a visit, for which Earlene would happily spend the entire morning and afternoon in the kitchen preparing a mouth-watering meal. Sundays, Earlene left for church at 9 AM, while Clyde remained at home in his chair, glued to Fox News. The threat of hell and damnation were no match for Election Year coverage. Sunday's choir rehearsal was followed by worship, and later, coffee fellowship. If she was fortunate, Clyde would get a hankering for a burger and the two would escape off to Hardee's for a brief and affordable Sunday lunch. After grilled cheese and soup for

Sunday dinner, they were in bed by 9 PM to set the alarm and start all over again. Lord willing.

As Earlene carefully proceeded up the steps to the back door of their modest home, she made sure to stamp off the snow from her boots before she went inside. She was greeted by none other than the droning background noise of Fox News.

"Hey, Hon', since you already have your boots on, you gonna shovel off the drive before bed?" Clyde bellowed from the living room.

Earlene's brow furrowed. She thought for a moment. Then spoke.

"I think not. Since I just got *in* from the cold, it's your turn to go *out* there and do it."

Silence. The creaking sound of Clyde rising from his chair was followed by some throat grumblings as he lumbered into the kitchen and appeared before his wife. They shared an equal sense of grumpiness.

"Tell you what," Clyde said as he parted the kitchen curtains to get a better look at the blustery snow. "How 'bout I tackle it in the morning? We're in for the night, right?"

"Just don't put it off. I can't be late for the bus to Charleston."

"Is that tomorrow?" Clyde asked snidely, as he poked his head into the fridge.

Earlene took off her coat and left her boots by the door. She stepped into her fuzzy slippers and stomped past her husband. He knew full well that she was leaving in the morning for her trip to Bermuda. A chartered bus would be departing from Bristol, taking passengers to Charleston, where they would board the *Princess of the Seas* for a magnificent, six-day, seven-night voyage for Bermuda. She could not wait, and no curmudgeon of a husband was going to stand in her way.

In the bedroom, Earlene dragged out an old hard-sided Samsonite suitcase. She'd had it since college. It had served her well on all her trips back and forth between Davidson and home. She clicked open the latch release, and the anticipation of travel ignited a special little flame of hope in Earlene. Personally, she thought it was a travesty that she had taught third graders for 35 years about the geography of the world, but she had not taken the time nor the money to explore it herself. "Time waits for no man," her mother often said. And those words resonated with Earlene now more than ever.

Earlene busied herself with packing. A light sweater for the cool nights at sea, a couple of pairs of capri pants, some summery tops, the cherry red micro-dotted sundress she had worn for Lisa's bridal shower, her famous red pumps, a week's worth of undergarments, a cotton nightgown, a one-piece swimsuit she'd ordered on-line from the Blair catalog, her sensible leather sandals, a pair of tennis shoes, and a couple pairs of socks. In her carry-on tote, Earlene prudently packed one pair of underwear, her toiletries, sunscreen, an umbrella (just in case), an Agatha Christie novel, her reading glasses, a small camera, a notebook, pen and pencil. She stepped out of her fuzzy slippers and tossed those in, too.

As she closed her suitcase, Clyde shuffled into the bedroom. She didn't bother to look in his direction. Clyde pulled the bedroom door partway shut and lifted Earlene's woven sun hat off a hook on the back of the door.

"I s'pose you'll be needing this where you're goin'," Clyde said solemnly.

"Why, yes!" Earlene replied with surprise. "Thank you for remembering."

"Sunscreen?" Clyde asked.

"Already packed."

"Tylenol? Baby aspirin?"

"Do you think I'll get too much exercise? Afraid my heart'll give out?"

"Honey, at our age, you never know what'll give out," Clyde reached for his wife's hand.

"Oh Clyde, it's just for one week. I'll be fine, and so will you." Earlene hesitated for a split second and then took hold of his big burly hand. The two sat on the edge of their bed.

"Do you still love me, Earlene?"

"This trip isn't about love. It's about sanity. After losing Mama, I realized I needed to do something for myself," she replied. "And by the way, my answer is yes. After forty-two years, I still love you, Clyde. But I need this. When's the last time we went on vacation?"

"What about Indianapolis, in twenty-twelve?"

"A weekend of burning rubber, screaming engines, and high speed mania is not *my* idea of a vacation. Maybe it is for you, but not for me. Besides, that was twenty-twelve!"

"Can we afford this?"

"Half of our retirement account belongs to me. By my calculations, I can afford it."

"Did you have to pick Bermuda? I mean a place like that, good golly! Sounds like you're up to something," Clyde mumbled with a hint of worry in his voice. "Maybe some hootchie-cootchie."

"Would that be so terrible? Maybe that tropical sun will bring back some hootchie-cootchie. There was a time when you seemed to like that about me."

Clyde grinned, devilishly. "Just as long as you bring it back to me, and nobody else."

"If you keep my kitchen clean, you've got yourself a deal."

Earlene and Clyde talked long into the night. She gave him full instructions on how to heat up all the meals she had prepared and sealed up in Tupperware in the fridge, along with plenty of biscuits wrapped in foil, and a new jar of strawberry jam set next to the coffee maker. She also told Clyde that Joey and Lisa planned to stop by on Thursday night to take him to Perkins for dinner. Clyde beamed like a boy on Christmas morning. She knew he was envisioning a big hearty slice of coconut cream pie for dessert. He coached her on how to use the tiny shower on the ship from his days of living on a destroyer when he served in the Navy. He also confessed that he was envious of all the food Earlene would be eating on the cruise. He had heard the buffets were fit for royalty. Clyde also suggested they stop by the drug store for Dramamine and Pepto-Bismol in the morning. As the winter wind howled outside their window, Earlene and Clyde huddled close to each other beneath the quilted covers and drifted off to sleep.

The next morning, Clyde was up before dawn. Earlene awoke to the roar of a snowblower. She dressed and found her passport beside her hairbrush on the dresser, where Clyde had thoughtfully placed it. With the SUV loaded up, they drove on through the snowy roads to town. In Bristol, Clyde pulled into the 24-hour Walgreen's parking lot. Earlene dashed inside to make her purchases. She surprised her husband with a Snicker's bar; he chuckled when she handed it to him. When they arrived at the travel agency, the chartered bus was parked nearby and passengers were boarding. Clyde parked and kept the engine running as he unloaded Earlene's suitcase and followed her to the bus.

Earlene was beginning to think that maybe she could use some baby aspirin. Her heart was racing. Her feet grew heavy and her steps slowed. Clyde took her by the arm and swiftly escorted her to the bus. Then Earlene did something she hadn't done in a long time. She kissed her husband. She felt his cold stubble against her lips. Clyde brought her in for a big hug, the kind of hug they used to share, long before Joey was born. The bus driver ushered the remaining passengers on board, and Earlene slowly broke free. She playfully blew Clyde a kiss and boarded the bus. With her heart and mind in check, Earlene was more than ready to say good-bye to the old routine and hello to sunshine and happiness.

The End

A Changed Woman

Linda Hudson Hoagland

Fairy tales hardly ever come true for quiet, fat girls. That is a fact.

I was the quiet, fat girl, the wall flower: that stick of furniture in the room that was always there, and definitely deserved no attention.

At least, that was what I *was*.

Now, I am before you a liberated woman: a writer, a mother, a widow, a retiree, and a size-18 person who enjoys life one day at a time.

In school, I was the short fat girl who had no friends—but that was the time I discovered what my calling was to be.

"Lady, who wrote these books?" asked a surly looking gentleman, who must not have noticed the nametag upon which my name was boldly printed, along with the title of author.

"I did," I answered.

"Tell me about that one," he said in a blustery, loud voice.

"Sure, I would love to. This story is about a young lady who was moved from a rural area of southern Ohio to the city of Cleveland, Ohio. It's the only one I have written that did not take place in southwest Virginia. I have lived in Stillwell County for over thirty years," I said. Before I could continue, he interrupted my onslaught of words with another question.

"Is that you? Are you writing about yourself?" he blurted out loudly.

I thought for a moment before I answered, "Yes sir, it is about me, and those I knew in the earlier part of my life."

"Then it is a true story?" he asked.

"Most of it is. I embellished it a bit in certain places, to make it more interesting," I explained.

"I've already read it, you know. You don't seem to have very many copies of that particular book for sale. Why is that?" he demanded,

"It's out of print. I'm selling what I have left," I said. I tried to end my conversation with him so others who were standing in front of me and listening to both of us could ask questions.

"Why are you letting it go out of print?" he asked.

"Because some of my readers called it trash, and others have called it the best book they have ever read. Some of those who called it trash are people with whom I want to remain friends," I answered.

"Why is it trash?" he continued.

"The main character, Ellen, lived in the inner city for ninety percent of the time she lived in Cleveland. She saw and did things most people in the small, rural towns of southwest Virginia only read about—and that reading is due to being forced, not by choice. As it turned out, the Bible belt was not the best place for my first book to be released. Now does anyone else have a question about my other books, perhaps?"

"So you *are* caving in; you're going to let it die. I have read most of your books, and that one is the best one you've written by far," said the surly man in a gentler tone.

"Why are you so interested in that book?" I asked. "I have written several others."

"Why did you write that one first? You obviously had many other stories to tell. Why that one first?" he continued.

9

"It was the one I had to write. I had to see it on paper. I had to see that the correct choice had been made, when Ellen left Cleveland behind her," I explained solemnly.

"Was it? The right choice, I mean," he probed.

"I didn't think so at first, because I was returning to a life I wasn't particularly happy with when I was a child. But I acclimated myself to honest, trusting, people once again, and now it is my home. It is my chosen home," I explained with a smile.

"Is that book going to be gone forever?" he asked.

"No sir; talking with you has made up my mind for me. I am going to rewrite the story, softening it to where the people in this area will accept it. It will be reissued in three volumes, a trilogy, and Ellen will become a hero—not the ordinary person she was in the first book," I said with a smile.

"It will no longer be true?" he asked.

"Yes sir—but it won't be as harsh and straightforward. It will hide some of the realities of the inner-city life, instead of throwing those realities into the face of the reader. Now—does anyone else have questions?" I asked as I tried to steer the conversation to another topic.

"When are you planning to do that, release the new books?" he asked.

"Probably next year. I have other writings that I am working on, and they must be tackled first," I said as pleasantly as I could. "Are there any more questions?"

When there were no takers, I sat down to sign the books for the people who were forming a line at the signing table.

The surly man stepped into the line at the end, holding my newest release.

I was talking with the people who were placing books to be signed by me in front of me much longer than usual. I really wanted the surly man to get discouraged and walk away from the line.

That didn't work. He eventually appeared before me, pushing my book in front of me for my signature.

"What is your name?" I asked.

"Robert Harrington," he replied.

I looked up at him with my mouth hanging open. When I finally closed my mouth, I asked, "Did you go the Lincoln High School in Cleveland, Ohio?"

"Yes, Ellen, we had a lot of classes together," the surly man replied.

"You've changed a lot," I said.

"Vietnam did that to me," he replied.

I checked to see if anyone else was standing behind him. I wanted to continue the conversation, now. I actually remembered who this man was, and I wanted to know why he was interrogating me so harshly.

"What are you doing in this area? It is so very different from the big city life of Cleveland, Ohio," I said.

"I was looking for you. I saw your picture by accident one day, and I went on from there. Your name was printed under the photograph as Ellen Hutchins Holcombe. I knew you as Ellen Hutchins. Your address is all over the Internet. That's dangerous, you know," he said with a smile.

"I know, but I have to remain reachable. I make my living doing what I am doing today," I answered. "Why were you looking for me? You hardly gave me the time of day when we were in high school."

"I was wrong then. I'm sorry about that," he said solemnly.

"But why me? What is it that you want?" I probed. I was not quite sure how to handle this.

"I want to ask you to dinner. I'm not a stranger. You know me from high school. I know that several years have passed, but I am still the same person now that I was then," he said as pleasantly as he could.

"How do you know I'm not married? How do you know I don't have a husband waiting for me in the car?"

"Your husband is deceased and has been for several years. I found that information on the 'Net. You might have a man friend, but I couldn't find that out. Do you? Do you have a man friend?" he asked.

"Let me think about it while I sign the books for the people standing behind you," I said, as I reached for the book a lady was waiting for me to sign.

My mind was spinning as I tried to figure out what I should do. Yes, I knew Robert Harrington, but that was 50 years ago. He could have become

11

a serial killer during that passage of the time. I knew I had changed a lot, from the wall flower that I used to be.

When it came time for me to pack up and leave, Robert Harrington was still there. He was standing over to the side, just barely out of sight, waiting for me to leave. I knew he would follow me out of the door.

I started walking toward the door and he was right behind me. He reached over to push the door open for me and waited for me to walk through to the outside.

Now what?

"Robert, where were you planning to go eat?" I asked.

"There's a good restaurant/bar combination in Stillwell, Donnie's Place. Do you know the place?" he asked.

"Yes, I've been there. It's a bit pricy, but they do have good food," I suggested.

"Good," he said.

"Why don't I meet you there? You can follow me or I can follow you back to Stillwell. It shouldn't take any more than an hour to get there, and we can get reacquainted," I offered, hoping he would consent so we could talk among others who would be in the establishment. It was a good hangout for those of the legal profession: lawyers, judges, and the like. I would feel a little better, more at ease, knowing there would be help available if I needed it.

He held the door while I climbed into my car. "Thank God," I mumbled as I started my engine. I was so grateful that nothing happened. He could have knocked me in the head and dragged me off to who knows where, and done who knows what.

I had been followed, perhaps I should say stalked, once before in my life that I was aware of. That experience ended well, and my stalker and I became good friends. He meant me no harm, but it was hard to realize that when he popped up everywhere I went. He left several little notes; I just misread them.

The situation was not the same with Robert. He was good at his task. I had no idea that he was following my every move. I had no idea that that

I had become his favorite search topic on the Internet. I had no idea what he wanted.

We drove on to Donnie's Place; all the while my mind searched for a reason for him to want to renew our acquaintance after so many years.

I pulled into the parking lot, with Robert following close behind me. The lot was full of cars, and I was truly glad to see that. I wanted many people in Donnie's Place, so there would be no chance of misbehavior without an audience.

Robert held the door for me as we entered the restaurant.

Our conversation was awkward. Besides the fact that we hadn't seen each other for 50 years, the music was so loud our speaking was held to a minimum.

We ordered dinner and I tried to relax.

When the waiter presented the bill for payment, Robert took it and pulled out a credit card.

"You don't have to pay for mine," I said not wanting to be obligated to him for anything—not yet, anyway.

"Of course I do. I asked you to dinner, and I will be the gentleman," he responded with a smile.

The smile did it. He looked like the Robert Harrington I knew 50 years ago, except he was grayer and had a few extra lines on his face.

"Robert, I'm going to have to go on home because I have an early appointment tomorrow morning. It was really good seeing you, and I hope I will run into you again," I said to my old friend.

"How about tomorrow?" he asked.

"No, I think not. Let's give it a couple to days to soak into our minds," I offered.

"Okay, that's fine," he said. "I'll call you in a couple of days."

I climbed into my car, pulled away from the parking lot, and headed for home. When I glanced into the rearview mirror, I didn't see his car behind me. I was afraid he would follow me home, and I wasn't ready for the confrontation.

13

I pulled my car into my driveway, and noticed someone sitting in a vehicle across the street from my house. He actually got to my house before I did. He was sitting there in his car, waiting for me to get home.

I ran into the house and reached for the telephone. I was going to dial 911, but I thought I should check out the window to see if he was still there.

He was gone.

My writer's imagination was blowing this all out of proportion. I knew I had to sleep on it. I had to put space between what I was thinking then and what I would think about it the next morning.

I climbed out of bed a couple of times during the night to look out my front window. He wasn't there; I was safe and sound in my little house.

I smiled when I remembered the crush I'd had on Robert when I was a teenager. *Dreams and fairy tales do come true*, was my last thought as I went back to sleep.

Life was good at the age of 67, in my little Town of Stillwell, Virginia.

The End

By the Light of the Moon

Charlotte H. Deskins

Aunt Hettie Bishop didn't know, for the life of her, what she was going to do about them hired girls.

She didn't want them, and she sure didn't need them. For almost five years now, ever since her husband's passing, she had lived up here on the highest ridge of Mountain Fork all alone, and doing for herself just fine. She made her own garden and tended her own house and barn. She had the company of the birds and the trees and the animals, which was just about all the socializing she could stand. She got along just fine.

But then, one day, just at sunset, in the fall of the year when the leaves were burnishing into gold and flame, here came that Preacher Martin puffing up the hill, dragging with him them two half-grown girls.

Aunt Hettie watched them struggling up the steep path from her front porch. One of them, the little dark-haired, skinny one, allowed herself to be led like a lamb going to slaughter. Her eyes were downcast and her hair was tightly braided against her head. Aunt Hettie was prepared not to even let them through the door, but then that girl looked up. Her eyes were sweet and kind and brown as a ripened nut, the exact same color as her late husband Joseph's eyes. She looked scared to death.

The other girl, the tall one, was struggling to pull her long, slender hand away from the preacher's sweaty hold. She was too pretty for her own good, and she knew it already. Race horse slim but finely muscled, and with firm rounded curves. Her dark red hair wound down her back like a waterfall made out of the colors of sunset. Her dark green eyes were narrow and cat-like. She was dressed older than her age of about 14, with little gold hoops in her ears. On her small feet were a pair of shiny black patent leather shoes, with kitten heels. She would have to get this one into practical mountain clothing soon.

Aunt Hettie never said a word, just stood there on the porch leaning a bit on her rush broom. The preacher hailed her. "Afternoon, Miz Bishop. This here's Jussie, and this here's Sal." He gestured first to the dark-haired girl, and then the redhead. "The elders of the church asked me to bring them up to you. They ain't got no family now, and we thought you could use some help up here all alone. They're right good workers, both of them. Ain't that right, girls?"

The silence was thick enough to cut with a blade. Aunt Hettie just stood there and let it sink in a little more. Silence had always been more friend than enemy to her. Jussie looked up hopefully. Sal ground the toe of her shoe into the grass. Finally, the preacher said, "Miz Bishop, we've come a long way up this mountain. Ain't you at least gonna ask us in for a drink?"

Aunt Hettie lifted her chin and said, "Well, come on in. I reckon I can spare a little water." She set the rush broom by the side of the door. Then she turned and went inside without looking back. They were left to follow in her wake.

Thirty minutes later, the preacher was walking quickly away from the cabin alone. He really wanted to get off that ridge before dark. Aside from the bobcats and the bears that roamed these high, lonely woods, he knew there were other even more fearful things. Haints that stirred the trees with their fingers like a cold wind. Hairy men with arms big around as a tree limb. Strange gold and green witchlights that played through the air here after dark. And then there were the Old Spirits, older than time, that liked to sing folks into a delirium so that they entered strange enchanted places, never to return. Oh, their body might come back, but their mind and spirit remained a prisoner in that far land forever. He'd been raised on these stories, same as everyone else.

He touched the buckeye he carried in his pocket for luck and as a guard against bewitchment. He also carried a gold cross and a tiny bottle of Holy Anointed Oil, just in case.

He felt a little guilty, leaving the girls up here with Aunt Hettie. He thought in truth she was just a lonely old woman. But there was more than one member of his church who whispered that witchery ran in her blood (on both sides, mind you) and that she could do strange things.

She could cure a fever just by laying hands on you. She could talk to the birds and animals and they would answer back, giving up the secrets of the mountain. It was whispered that she often walked alone, beneath the waxing moon, and that when she did, the Powers of Old rained down upon her. Some said she even could even speak with the devil, although why anyone would want to do that he couldn't imagine. He quickened his pace. His work here was done.

As the weeks passed, the girls settled in to earning their keep. Sal, although lazy to a fault, turned out to be a good cook. Her stews and cornbread were a real treat. Jussie could do just about anything. No job was beneath her. She fed the animals, milked the cow, fed the sheep, and used the wash board and cook stove with ease. She scrubbed the privy and helped Hattie burn off the old garden and bury the last of the apples for winter. She hummed softly as she sat by the fire at the end of the day, mending an apron or hemming up some dresses Hettie had given them.

The girls shared a large loft above Hettie's bedroom. She could hear them whispering before they went to sleep. She did not feel one bit bad about this; it gave her insight into these two strangers that she had taken in.

Jussie wanted desperately to be liked by Sal, who took advantage of the younger girl, getting her to do any chores she was not inclined to do. She was often cruel to Jussie, mocking her for her dry, cracked hands.

The next time Jussie went out to milk the cow, Hettie took her aside and handed her a small bottle. "It's rose water and glycerin," she told the girl. "Rub it over your hands and face each night. And every time you feed the sheep and lambs, run your hands through their wool. It'll soften them." Jussie obeyed, and soon her skin looked much better. Hettie also gave her some grape vine juice for her hair, and told her to loosen the tight braids. She began to look almost as pretty as Sal, but Sal would never admit it.

Once a week, she took them down the mountain to town. She was no longer as agile as she was in younger days. There was a rickety, swinging bridge they had to cross; Sal would always take Hettie by the arm and help her across. Hettie hoped that might be a good sign about the girl.

In town, they bought the week's provisions—salt, fine thread for mending, coffee—things not easily made on Mountain Fork. Hettie saw how much the girls loved candy, so she made sure they each got their favorites to take home. Hard raspberry for Jussie and flat chocolate discs sprinkled with little white dots for Sal. On one cold trip to town, she took out her most prized possession, a silk scarf given to her by Joseph on their wedding day. It was green with yellow roses scattered across it.

Sal drew in her breath when she saw it. "Why, Miz Bishop; what a lovely scarf!" She drew one long slender finger across it. Hettie felt a chill run down her back right between her shoulder blades.

That night, as she lay listening to their soft voices rising and falling, she heard Jussie say, "Sal, take that off! What would Miz Hettie say if she caught you?"

There was low, derisive laughter from Sal. "She'll never know. Not unless you tell her. I'll put it back before she misses it! Besides, it looks much better on me than on her frizzy ole gray head! The green of it brings out my eyes, don't you think?" Hettie crept to the dresser and silently slid open the drawer where she kept her scarf. Sure enough, it was gone.

"Besides, I always was meant for nicer things. Who knows? This pretty thing may well be mine for good, before too long."

"What do you mean, Sal?"

"Oh, it wouldn't take much. I might just have to put a little poison in her stew before too long, if she keeps working us like she has been these last few weeks." She gave a low, dark laugh.

"Oh, Sal! Please, promise me you won't. I like Miz Bishop. You could like her, too, if you'd just let yourself."

Sal did not answer.

That's when Hettie knew she had to do something about them girls.

They made plans for one more trip to town before the truly cold weather set in. It was closing in toward Christmas, so Hettie gave the girls a little money to buy gifts for one another while she did a little business of her own in town. In one more week, the moon would be waxing and they would make the trip down.

In the meantime, she began to look at the moon each night. She gathered such herbs and yarbs as she needed from her storeroom. Hettie began to slip out at night while the girls slept, wandering in the woods, only returning as the morning light crept over the cabin. She was bathed and glowing with moonlight.

Ever since the night she had heard them talking, Sal was no longer allowed near the cooking. Hettie made all the tea for the three of them to drink as they sat around the fireplace before bed.

Soon the time came around for their last trip to town before the holidays. Hettie took Jussie aside and handed her an envelope. "Here, take this with you," she told the girl. "Keep it hid from Sal. You and Preacher Martin hand it over to the lawyers in town, first thing in the morning. They'll know what to do for you."

The girl's eyes filled with tears. "I don't want anything bad to happen to you, Miz Bishop. You've always been good to me." She hesitated. "There's something you need to know."

"Hush now," Hettie said. "Try not to worry. I'm sure all will turn out for the best."

They made their way down the mountain with Hattie wearing her scarf. It had miraculously reappeared in her drawer the next day. She said nothing as Sal took her arm, and she allowed the girl to guide her across the bridge. Each of the girls went separate ways to shop for their gifts after

Hettie told them where to meet back up for the trip home. When Sal arrived, it was almost dusk. She was surprised to see only Hettie waiting for her. "Jussie is staying the night with the preacher's family," the older woman said. "It's just you and me tonight, Girl." Sal said nothing. She seemed as calm and serene as a hen in a nest; yet Hettie could feel the greed and envy pouring out of her.

As they made their way toward the swinging bridge, night seemed to swoop down upon them. The two women huddled together against the cold wind. The waxing moon and the stars looked sharp enough to slice yourself on them. Just as they reached the middle of the bridge, Sal reached over and snatched the scarf from the old woman's head.

"It ain't right, you havin' such a nice thing!" she cried. "It ain't right, you havin' everything there is and me with nothin'!" She shoved Hettie over the edge of the bridge, toward the icy water. The old woman just managed to grip the rotting slats and hold on. "Don't you do this, Sal Ramsay," she begged. "I've talked with Him about you, but the deal is far from done. You can still save yourself. Help me up, and let's us go on home now." Hettie looked deep into the girl's green eyes. "Please, Sal, help me up and let's just go on home. We need never speak of this night again."

Sal seemed to consider for a moment, but then her eyes hardened and frosted over with hate. "No, I like my plan better!" She started to pull Hettie's hands away from the planks as the icy river sang for its sacrifice below.

Instead of fighting her, Hettie leaned up close with the last of her strength. She said, "Then the devil take you, Sal Ramsay, by the light of the waxing moon, and fly with you straight into hell. You will sit by his side and drink from his cup and have all you want of riches and finery. But it will bring no happiness to you, not in all eternity."

Sal gave another tug, and Hettie's hands at last gave up the boards. She plummeted into the rolling water below, her cry an echo in the winter air. Then all was silent. Sal sat back on her heels and admired her prize. The scarf wound through her hands like warm water over a stone. She held it up as a screen between her and the fading moon.

And then she saw him. A dark figure between herself and the moon. He was huge and manlike, but for the two large twisting horns that rose out of his head and the evil grin that split his face. He wrapped her up in his strong scaly arms, and she felt the harsh kiss of leathery wings against her face. She struggled and screamed, but all her words were drowned out by the river and captured by the boughs of the evergreen trees that grew along the bank.

Early the next morning, Jussie came up the path leading both the town lawyer and Preacher Martin. She had done just as Hettie instructed, and opened the documents with both of them as her witnesses. A quarter mile past the river, they found the frozen body of Hettie Bishop washed up out of the river, wedged against an oak tree.

Of Sal Ramsay, there was no sign, except for a single, beat-up black patent leather shoe. Its heel was broken. They tried to get Jussie to come back with them to the safety of the town, but she refused. The lawyer silently handed her the copy of Hettie's notarized will, leaving everything to Jussie. The men took the body back down with them to the funeral parlor, and left Jussie alone to make her way back to her cabin up on the ridge.

Just before she reached the rock path that led to the place she now owned, free and clear, something caught her attention. There, fluttering on a branch, was the green silk scarf with yellow roses. Jussie reached up and pulled it free. She folded it up carefully. She took it home and buried it by the front door, hoping she had done the right thing.

The following spring, she got her answer. A plant pushed up through the sun-warmed earth where she had buried the scarf. It had leaves as shiny and soft as green silk. Soon it filled with buds; when they opened, each one was a yellow rose, lit from within by something that looked a lot like moonlight.

The End

Climbing a Ladder with Thorns

Katie Meade

Enjoying the warm sun and cool breeze, Kate—as usual—was involved in brain-storming for her next book. Although Kate lived a comfortable life in Virginia, where she grew up, life had not always treated her with such generosity. Kate often thought of her childhood when she was alone with her thoughts. She had been raised in a coal camp located in Virginia, along with her other siblings. Although she had been raised in a family with love and kindness, Kate's life had been filled with hardships and emotional turmoil.

The night was dark and stormy when Kate made her entrance into the world. That night seemed a prelude to the harsh life she would have to endure over the course of the next 20 years. Born in 1948 to a family living only on what her father could manage to work out as a coal miner was not a great start for a baby—especially a girl. Kate's father and mother, along with their families, had lived and worked in an Appalachian coal camp for three generations. Although Kate was the first child of Katheryn and

Stanley Nash, and the first maternal grandchild, her chances at overcoming the adversity and poverty she was born into seemed impossible. Kate would grow up feeling each thorn on the ladder she had to climb. Her only hope lay in becoming tough, gaining courage, and relying on her wits as she grew up in the coal camp in Virginia.

After Kate was born, her mother Katheryn (for whom she was named) gave birth to a new baby every year—or maybe two years, if she was lucky. Kate's mother had endless chores to do every day. Therefore, by the time Kate was four, her job was to play with the other babies who were old enough to sit tied into a small chair with a diaper. It was necessary for Kate to help watch the babies. Kate and her family lived with her grandparents David and Mary, so occasionally an aunt would show up to visit and help with the babies. This helpful gesture gave Kate time to spend with Grandpa David, who was her very favorite person.

Grandpa David did not expect Kate to do chores or run errands for him. On the contrary, he just wanted to spend time with her. Grandpa would take Kate fishing for catfish or other aquatic life that lived in the creek that ran by their house. Finding a huge crawdad to bring home made the splash in the creek even better. Sometimes Grandpa would read to Kate from books that he had borrowed or purchased from the rag store where the family usually bought their clothes. This was one of the highlights of the day for Kate. Usually, the book was read after the day was done and everyone was resting after supper. An oil lamp had to be used because electricity was not available nor affordable for Kate's family. Reading by the oil lamp made Kate sleepy and gave her a feeling of contentment. Kate's grandpa was the stability in her life. Each time Grandpa read to Kate, she was always left with the satisfying thought that someday she would be able to read on her own.

Kate didn't live far from her paternal grandparents and other relatives, but she didn't enjoy going to visit them. It seemed that everyone except her Grandpa David and Grandma Mary always had chores for her to do, which included little fun time. By the time Kate was five, she gathered eggs, fed the chickens, and helped with her other siblings. So, going where there were still more chores did not appeal to the child within her. However,

Kate still went to help her grandparents on a regular basis. Grandma Bell did tell Kate stories about her great grandpa, and how her ancestors had come from England and Ireland. Grandma Anna did occasionally take Kate to the Rag Store to buy her a new dress. Sometimes she even bought candy for her at the Ben Franklin. These were special days for Kate.

Grandma Mary and Kate's mother often spoke of Grandma's brother Henry, who lived in West Virginia. Kate could not remember when Uncle Henry had ever come to visit them. However, a letter came from Henry one day, saying he was going to come visit for a whole week. Everyone was excited when Henry arrived. Kate was overwhelmed when Henry picked her up and hugged her. He drove a white convertible, something that was totally new to Kate. She had never seen a car without a top. Kate and her siblings got into the car to sit for a short while. After a time, everyone settled down and a special meal was cooked for Henry.

Over the next three days, Kate became acquainted with Henry and found that she enjoyed his company. On the day that Henry left, he asked Kate if she would like to go for a ride in his car without a top. Jumping into the front seat of the car, Kate had never felt so excited or special. Henry asked Kate if she wanted to take the side road, where other vehicles did not go because of the rough terrain. Kate agreed with her uncle, and before long, he was driving on a bumpy road. Kate was so interested in riding in Henry's car that she didn't care where they went. This was her first ride in such a strange car.

When Henry pulled over and stopped the car Kate wondered what was wrong. Before she had time to ask, she was overtaken by Henry's arms. He pulled Kate's small body toward him and kissed her on the mouth. This made Kate feel funny, because even her mom and dad didn't kiss her like this. Henry told Kate that everything was OK because he was her uncle, and he loved her. Feeling overwhelmed, Kate started to protest but Henry's hands found other places besides her shoulders to clutch. Kate wiggled from his grasp and started to cry. She pressed her whole body against the door, as far away from him as she could get. Henry just swore and started the car. Kate and Henry never spoke again, while they were driving back home or otherwise. Kate ran off to play when Henry stopped the car.

Grandma Mary loved her brother, so Kate would keep secret the terrible way Henry touched her, making her feel like she had done something terribly wrong.

Kate was quiet and often spent time alone for the next few weeks. Moreover, she would grow up having to deal with Henry's violation. Just a few months after Henry left the coal camp where Kate's family lived, he was killed in a terrible mining accident. The accident happened right before he planned on coming back to visit with Kate's family. Henry's family grieved in a terrible way after he died. Grandma Mary cried for days over the loss of her brother. Kate just looked at Henry's still body, glad that he would never bother her again. Kate would continue to keep her terrible secret, because her family believed Henry was a good man. No one, especially her family, would believe what Henry had done to her when she took the ride with him.

Years passed in the coal camp. Kate had learned to push thoughts of the ride with Henry to the back of her mind. Life for the family went on as usual; it just wasn't the same for Kate. Crops were harvested and canned for the winter, which kept the whole family busy. In the autumn, after temperatures dropped, the hogs were slaughtered. Christmas in Appalachia came and went, with the usual treats and small presents. Kate enjoyed life with her family, especially fishing with her father and helping Grandpa David shell corn, which always included good stories. Kate's interaction with her family over the years set a foundation that would help Kate overcome obstacles in her life and eventually become successful in her endeavors.

Kate didn't start school until she was seven, because the country school was too far for her to walk. Now, Kate and her sister Janice, who was six, would start together. Kate excelled in school without any problems. Kate was overjoyed when she found out that the teacher had books that she could borrow and read. School was a place where Kate found an outlet from her monotonous life in the coal camp. However, she had hardly begun her school adventure when her parents had to move for her father to keep work. The move was just a few miles away, but the community had a different community school. Although Kate did not like having to change schools, she quickly adjusted, made new friends, and continued to excel in her studies. Kate would end up going to five different schools within the region before she started high school at the age of 15.

By the time Kate entered high school, her father was disabled and no longer worked. He had barely escaped death when a huge rock fell on him while he was working his normal shift in the coal mine. Over the next few years, Kate's family suffered the adjustment of living on social security instead of a regular miner's pay. Living in the Appalachians meant there was always a garden, along with chickens and hogs to live on. Kate knew her father well enough to know that the family would always be provided for. Provision for the family, however, meant wearing used clothes bought from the community rag store. Moreover, clothes brought to the family by a neighbor was always a welcome event. Kate's mother made some of the clothes that the seven children of the family woe using blue flowered chop sacks; her mother also used these chop sacks to make sheets for the beds. Kate's mother always used anything that could be recycled. The family way of living did not change much even after Kate became older. This was just the way her family lived.

Kate's high school experience was very different than what she had been accustomed to. Most of the students had gone to a larger city school from the start of their school career. Compared to the other kids, Kate stood out as a country bumpkin. Although Kate made good grades, she had few good friends. The one friend that she did have was killed by a drunk driver when she was 15. Tina's death just added to the negative things that Kate had to deal with. Although Kate was lonely, she found solace with her family and church, where she and her mother were active. Kate had become an avid reader over the course of her school career, reading at least three books a week. Moreover, she had written and directed a church play at the age of fourteen. Although Kate remained troubled over the past events of her life, she had learned to go forward. She would never reveal her dark secret to anyone.

When Kate was 17, life threw her another terrible curve. Just at the time when she was getting close to her mother, she lost her to a massive heart attack. Kate's father was devastated by the loss of his wife. Turning to alcohol, Kate's father stayed in such an unstable and emotional state that she was left with the chore of taking care of her family. There was, however, one stable factor left in Kate's life. Brad and Kate had met at a school ball game when she was 16. Since that time, Brad had been a regular visitor at her house. Kate knew that she could rely on his support, no matter what life threw her way. Kate felt a sense of gladness that her mother had approved of Brad. She just waited patiently for her father to regain control of his life; Kate knew her father well enough to know that he would find the strength to overcome his grief.

Although Kate's father was starting to deal with his grief, Kate realized that she would not be able to stay in school and take care of the family. Dropping out of school her junior year broke both her and Brad's heart. Kate's father did not see the need for her to remain in school, especially with such a large family to care for. However, Brad felt the opposite; he wanted Kate to pursue what she loved best, an education and writing. Kate would have to feel her way through life with Brad, who was the love of her life. Kate had lost her Grandma Mary a few years before her mother died. Moreover, her Grandpa David now lived with one of his other daughters and her family. The strength and comfort that she had drawn from him was now far away, especially since she had no telephone to call him. However, Brad stood as a strong tree for Kate to lean on. When all was said and done, Brad would always be the stability in Kate's troubled life.

Only a few months had passed when Kate wished she had never dropped out of school. Her father had met another woman, and decided to marry her after just a short time. Kate felt strange when her father's new bride Betty came to live with them. At first, Betty seemed very pleasant and agreeable. Moreover, Betty started completing a lot of the household chores. For the most part, the family seemed to get along well. However, life soon changed where Betty was concerned. Over the next few months, the new mother changed dramatically. Betty seemed to have an awakening after a time of working to take care of a large family. She started a strict regimen of assigning chores and making sure they were carried out. Kate, or any one of the other kids who dared to cross her, suffered the discipline of her father when he learned of their offense. This was the life Kate and her siblings would live until they left home.

Kate and Brad decided to get married in the spring of 1967. Before Kate was 20, she had her first baby—another followed just three years later. Although Kate and Brad were happy with their family, she still wanted to pursue a formal education. When her children were a few years old, Kate started working toward her diploma, finishing in only a year. Brad then encouraged Kate to start college classes at a local university. Although Kate was hesitant, she eventually put her foot through the door of a classroom, where she started what ended up as a teaching career in English. However, the diploma that she worked for did not come easy. Again, Kate had to juggle her family and kids' activities, and still find time to go to school and study. She found herself up many days before 5 AM, studying for exams or completing school work. In the end, all was accomplished and Kate received her college degree.

Over the course of her teaching career, Kate found herself keeping a journal and writing poems. By the time her career was over, her writing grew in diversity. Finally, at the encouragement of her friends and family, she decided to publish one of her books. Surprisingly, the novel she had written sold better than she had expected. Kate sent one of her books to a publisher, which propelled her to bestselling status. Finally, Kate rejoiced in her life accomplishments. Nobody, not even Kate, had expected the girl from the coal fields of Virginia to overcome her many hardships, have a successful career, and become a well-known author.

Basking in the sun, Kate realized that days like the present were her best days. She no longer worried much about her past. Realizing that the thorny ladder that she had climbed while growing up had only served to make her strong and able to endure the inevitable curves of life. Kate now lived a life free of any thought that she was the cause of any dark events of her life. Now, Kate focuses on her present life and the abundant joy that perseverance brings.

The End

Snowflakes

Susan Robinson Butler

I stared out the window, lost in thought, watching dozens of snowflakes cascade to the ground, covering the grass in a soft, white blanket. They say that every snowflake is different; if you examined it with a microscope, you could see a unique pattern. Well, for me, every snowflake is a memory: a representation of a moment in time. And at this particular moment, I was reminded of the day my grandmother went to join the Lord.

It was the first day of spring, on a day much like this one. I looked out the window of a modest hospital room as massive snowflakes fell to the ground, covering the parking lot and cars in frozen crystals. I saw the familiar water tower looming over the quaint little town nestled high in the Appalachian Mountains of Southwest Virginia. I watched as the last remnants of Old Man Winter showed himself; much like my grandmother, he was not going out without a fight. The room was quiet, other than Grandma Ivy's shallow breathing and the hum of the machines monitoring her vital signs.

As I sat in my living room on a cold winter's day nearly 20 years later, I was reminded of that time, when I watched my grandmother take her last breath. A single mother, dutiful grandmother, loving sister, and compassionate friend—she was all of that and more. I was reminded of the strong Appalachian woman that she was all of her life.

Ivy raised her daughter without the help of her mother, who had died when my mother was an infant. My grandmother continued to live at her childhood home, caring for both her father and her daughter.

After her father's death, Ivy took over all of the duties of the tiny farm. She grew corn, beans, and potatoes. She carried buckets of water from the spring, and canned the vegetables in a washtub over an open fire. She gathered eggs for breakfast, and on special occasions, Ivy killed a chicken, plucked it, then cut it up for frying. Trips to the store were rare, as they either walked or caught a ride from one of the few neighbors who owned a car. I felt humbled as I looked out the window at our family's two vehicles, now covered in the fresh, powdery snow.

As I continued to watch the snowflakes fall to the ground and coat the tops of the trees, I began to see each one as a memory of happier times. I believe that the best way to keep our loved ones with us after they are gone is to honor their memory. I will never forget those small moments, which stand out in my mind like a beacon of light in a sea of storm clouds. I have already begun to tell my children stories about their great-grandmother, the feisty mountain woman they never got a chance to meet.

As I stared out at the falling memories, I reached out and plucked one from the air. It took me back to a hot summer's day in the holler, at the old home place that had been my Grandma Ivy's dwelling since birth. In that memory, I looked around the one bedroom house with wonder. Even as a ten-year-old girl, I was drawn to the memories of that sanctuary, nestled between two fresh mountain streams. In the wintertime, smoke billowed out of the chimney from the black coal stove that sat in the living room. Visitors crossed the stream via a small wooden bridge that followed a worn path through a gate and up the painted wooden steps that led to the front porch. The long covered porch housed a brightly-painted red swing, which was my grandmother's favorite spot in the evenings. We spent many hours there, side by side, feeling the cool mountain breezes on our cheeks, watching the orange glow from the sun as it disappeared behind two peaks. A rickety old wooden outhouse stood behind the house as a reminder of another time. By the time I came around, it served as a storage shed for the lawnmower.

In my mind, I swayed in the porch swing, looking out past the freshly mowed green grass and the yellow marigolds in their white painted planters, made from old tires, to the majestic blue mountains that lay beyond the holler. I opened the creaky screen door and walked to the kitchen, towards the aroma of home-cooked food. I watched as my grandmother stirred a pot of chicken and dumplings for supper. It didn't matter to her that it was only ten in the morning. I had stood outside with her half an hour earlier as she watched the horizon from the back porch.

"Them's storm clouds a-comin'," she would say with a furrowed brow. "Gotta git that chicken on 'fore it gits here."

Used to this routine, I would simply sigh and say, "Okay, Grandma." Besides, I could eat her chicken and dumplings any time of day. Mama said I ate a whole pot by myself once at the age of two. She remembered because she and Daddy left me with Grandma to go to the World's Fair in '82.

The two of us had just finished our early lunch when we heard a distant rumble. I began to put on my shoes, as I had this routine down pretty well. My grandmother and I began the short walk up the dirt road to her sister's house. A fear of storms still runs in our family, but the two ladies were content to sit on the front porch together, watching the rain fall and telling tales of days gone by. I listened intently as I sat by my grandmother on the porch swing, as the storm clouds rolled in, covering the mountains in a thick, hazy fog.

"You 'member that time you were comin' up here with Peggy Mae, and y'all saw that big snake layin' cross the road?" Great-aunt Rachel began as she smoothed her apron. Her white hair was pulled back into a tight bun. She was tall and thin, with pale blue eyes that twinkled when she laughed. She reached into her apron pocket and pulled out her can of snuff. After placing the tobacco in her lip, she continued. "'Twas a hot day, 'bout like this one."

"Yeah, 'twas a copperhead too!" Grandma Ivy shook her head. "Peggy Mae just hopped right on over it like it was a stick of wood."

"And you was so scairt you wouldn't come any further." My aunt laughed heartily, then spit her tobacco into the cup that sat beside her rocking chair.

"So, what did you do, Grandma?" I asked curiously.

"I turned around and came back to the house. That's what, child. Your crazy mother jumped back across that snake and ran home with me. She couldn't have been much older than you are now." Ivy smiled at me fondly. My mother didn't share her mother's phobias.

According to my grandmother, her daughter was a free spirit—except, she would never put it that nicely. "I could never do a thing with that child. She made mud pies and climbed trees. Played in them woods day in and day out."

I knew from my mother's stories that she did a lot more than just play. I grabbed another memory from a snowflake that landed on the windowsill as I sipped my coffee. I pictured my mother telling me about her childhood as she folded a basket of laundry. "I was carrying buckets of water from the spring and washing clothes on a washboard before I was big enough to reach the sink. Had to stand in a chair." Used to hard work, even to this day, my mother is happiest while she is doing laundry, cleaning, or mowing the lawn.

"We took care of each other back then," she continued, "because there was nobody else around to do it." My mother never knew her father, but she never needed one. She learned to take care of herself at a young age.

I went to the kitchen to refill my cup and look out at the snow piled onto the deck. My eyes were drawn to another snowflake, and I was once again with my grandmother on her sister's front porch. After the storm was over, we said our goodbyes and began the trek back home. The air smelled new and fresh after the rain had washed everything clean. As we walked, my grandmother began to tell me another story about my mother, and how much spunk she had as a young woman.

"When your mother was little, she had a dog named Skip. He was black and white, and the smartest, prettiest dog you ever did see. Your mother even had that dog carrying the mail back to the house between his teeth. One day, these old boys came along and decided they wanted that dog. Well, your mother, she prolly loved that dog more than she did me and she worn't about to let some strangers run off with him, so you know what she did?" I looked up at her and shook my head. "She run inside the house and come back with a pistol. She fired off a shot clean over their heads, and they took off a-runnin' down that road faster than a shot out of a cannon. Never seen those boys 'round here no more after that." As she laughed, I was amazed by my mother's courage. I couldn't imagine living so far back in the holler that if you called 911, it would take at least an hour to reach you. Most people still drove themselves to the hospital, if it came to that.

We went inside the house and sat down. I asked my grandmother if she would play me a song. As she went into the bedroom to get her guitar, I looked around the room, taking in the old coal stove where she would sit and warm my hands in the winter, and the hodgepodge of what-nots that sat on the small wooden coffee table. I knew that although they didn't look valuable to me, each item held a special memory for my grandmother, of her mother and the family of nine children that had once lived within those four walls. I saw my grandmother's shotgun standing in the corner of the room, a smiley face sticker on the barrel, as if to warn any trouble-makers, *Go on, make my day.*

My grandmother came back and sat down with her favorite red guitar and began to play. She and I sang "Cripple Creek" and a lot of other Appalachian folk songs for hours. When we couldn't remember all of the verses, we just started back at the beginning. I smiled as I watched that petite, wiry woman with wavy, jet-black hair and sparkling blue eyes, her calloused fingers flying across the strings of the guitar. For Ivy, each note was like a memory of times gone by, when she would play with her brothers, sisters, and friends that had long since passed away.

Ivy kept on playing, smiling, and making memories to share with future generations. Now I know that she was leaving me memories: stories to pass down from generation to generation about life in a different time—

perhaps a simpler time, before Netflix streaming, video games, and social networking.

    I stood up and took my empty cup into the kitchen, placing it in the sink, transfixed by all the different snowflakes as I peered out the kitchen window. I wondered which ones I would be remembered in someday, when my children and grandchildren look out at the memories and pluck one from the air.

The End

I Promised

Sharyn Martin

Harber Steffey walked slowly away from the newly-covered grave. Five of his six children followed him; the baby, Lucinda, was staying with the Addington family. Harber's wife, Eliza, had suffered for a week. It was early September, 1918, and the three-day fever that had overrun the mountains in the spring had resurfaced as a killer illness.

Gilaney Addington was almost 16. She could handle baby Lucinda as well as anybody, according to her mother.

"You could do worse than Harber Steffey. He's goin' to need somebody to help him with them kids. You put on that yeller dress you made for church. Set out yonder on the porch. He'll be comin' back up here any time to get this young'n. He said he'd be here Wednesday, and it's Wednesday. Now you get out yonder."

Gilaney stepped behind the muslin curtain that offered small privacy to the two-room house. The yellow dress was hanging on a nail. It offered little brightness in the dark, drab room she shared with her twin sisters, thirteen, and five-year-old brother. She slipped off the wool shift and took the yellow dress. It felt strangely, wonderfully cool to her skin.

Harber walked up the path from the creek. The beauty surrounding him could just as well have been dry and barren as he was thinking how he could take care of these six children. Maybe the Addingtons would take Lucinda and raise her. If Eliza hadn't died, he wouldn't be faced with this. Farming was hard enough on this mountain. Never mind the extra burdens.

"Hail, house," he called as he neared the Addington clearing.

"Mr. Steffey," Gilaney replied in greeting. "You doin' alright now?"

"Just fair, ma'am. Just fair. Don't know hardly what I'm goin' to do. Got a family that needs raisin' and now Eliza's gone, I don't rightly know how I'm goin' do that."

Corda Addington listened in the shadows of the front room. She patted her hair and stepped out onto the porch. "How do, Harber. Are you makin' it alright? Guess you want the baby so's you can take her back. I reckon Gilaney could come down there two, three times a week and help out. 'Course, I need her here some 'til her Pa gets back. He should be back here in a week or so."

"I'd be grateful of the help, Corda. Maybe she could come down tomorrow, and be back here before dark."

The sun just barely peered through the trees when Gilaney started down the mountain. The Steffey place was out the road, just past the creek. Gilaney heard every sound as she went down the path; the squirrels and birds were busy.

"Hail, house", she called from the yard. Moses Steffey, the middle boy, came out to the porch. "Pa, Gilaney Addington is here."

"How do, Gilaney. Come on in. You can see what needs doin'. I'll be back up in the field, and you can send Moses after me if you need anything."

Gilaney set about putting the place in order. The fire was already going in the cookstove, so she got a bucket of water from the pump outside and brought it in to heat. Dishes and then the floor had to be washed. She looked around for something to fix for dinner. Mr. Steffey and five children had to be fed.

"Moses, go get your Pa. Dinner will be ready by the time you get back down here. Get the rest of the young'ns in here."

Gilaney rocked Lucinda for a few minutes and put her back in her cradle.

"Lord, bless this food and your bounty. Amen".

Dinner was quiet. Harber didn't allow talking at the table. When he was finished, he got up from the table and went outside. Gilaney could see him walking back to the field.

It was almost six o'clock when Gilaney came back up the mountain.

"Well, how did it go?" Corda asked her daughter.

"Ma, they're quare and Mr. Steffey ain't got a whole lot to say. The young'ns is the same way. They just look at me, and if I tell them to go outside, they go. They don't never say anything".

"Well, it could be worse. They could act like a bunch of wild uns, but I guess they're gettin' over their Ma being gone. You be nice, now, and do whatever you can to help Harber Steffey."

Gilaney walked down the mountain many times that fall to help Harber Steffey.

The day after Thanksgiving brought a big snow. The tree branches cracked and broke under the white weight. Harber Steffey waited 'til the ground cleared, then crossed the creek to the mountain path. He needed to talk to the Addingtons.

"Would you all be willing to let Gilaney marry me?" he asked as they sat around the hearth. "I need her help, and she's a good worker."

Gilaney listened from behind the muslin curtain. *He didn't say nothin' about loving me*, she thought.

"That'd be fine, but she ain't got nothin' to bring," Corda said. Burgess Addington didn't say anything. His wife done most of the talking, and since he was gone so much, he reckoned she figured she run the place.

"I reckon we got most of what she needs. Do you think we can be married by this Saturday?"

Gilaney Rebecca Addington Steffey. What a strange sound it made in her head. That's who she was now.

Corda had not told her daughter too much about marrying. Gilaney was not prepared for the pain to herself and the lack of feeling from Mr. Steffey. *Reckon this goes along with the helping,* she thought. He expected Gilaney to be agreeable to his every wish, and to be obedient to his demands.

The river sand rocks made good scrubbing tools for Gilaney. Kneeling on the wooden floor of the small house, she grasped the small rock and scrubbed back and forth. Finishing that chore, she grabbed the water bucket. Washing had to be done before noon so she could hang the clothes on the line to dry before supper. The wet clothes nearly froze to her hands in the icy mountain air. Pale winter sun didn't offer much heat.

The small church down the road welcomed the Steffey family Sunday morning. Preacher Campbell came through every month to minister to the folks on the mountain and down the valley road. He preached long, strong sermons about sin and hellfire, damning the sinners and praising the saints. The saints were only the few he approved of, and those who provided for his wellbeing. Gilaney shut her eyes and rocked quietly back and forth on the hard bench. She prayed to God for strength to endure the thankless life she had been given. She had learned that she had little will of her own anymore, leaving the mountainside home where her mother ruled, then going to a loveless marriage where her only purpose was to keep a clean house and care for six children—then subject herself to Harber Steffey.

"Gilaney, come here. I don't feel too pert." Harber rolled from one side to the other on the straw tick. Gilaney saw the sweat on his face and felt his forehead. His skin was clammy and sallow. His voice sounded weak and scratchy. Elderberry wine was the only medicine in the house. She gave him two spoonfuls, and he slept fitfully.

The nearest doctor was in Moccasin Gap, a seven-mile walk from home. Gilaney didn't know what else to do. Her Ma had made her promise she would help Mr. Steffey, and now she was married to him. The help she could provide was to go get the doctor.

Gilaney put on Harber's wool overcoat, tied on a scarf, and started her walk to Moccasin Gap. The wind was bitter and the snow flying. She just knew Harber had the fever that killed Eliza, and she had to get help. She had promised. She struggled to keep walking against the wind. Maybe it wasn't too much farther.

Dr. Ford's office was on the main street. He packed his bag, then he and Gilaney Steffey climbed into the buggy. Gilaney was so cold and tired. She welcomed the buggy ride and not having to walk back in the snow and wind.

Dr. Ford stayed the night with Harber Steffey, and Gilaney was right there beside him. Harber's fever broke in the morning and he asked for water. "I think he'll be all right," Dr. Ford told her.

Harber grew stronger every day, and was out of bed in less than a week. Gilaney felt she had kept her promise. She had helped Mr. Steffey. She was feeling poorly herself, though, and the cough she had taken after the long walk to Moccasin Gap had gotten worse. By the end of the second week, Gilaney was feverish and talking out of her head. She kept talking about promises, yellow dresses, and birds.

The small cross in the Lawson Confederate Memorial Cemetery was hand-carved: *Gilaney Rebecca Addington Steffey 1902–1918*.

The End

A Kindred Spirit

Susan Harmon

Julie held his cold hand. His skin felt rubbery. She watched John's face drain of any expression, his eyes staring past her as if mesmerized by something or someone. The doctor had given him a month to get his affairs in order—the old ticker was simply worn out. John's lips moved for words not uttered. Kneeling in front of him as he slumped in his wooden rocker, she told him how much she loved him. That was all she could think of to say to her partner of decades. In a second of silence, John left her. Julie waited for Gabriel's horn or the songs of the angels, but all she heard was the faint echo of a coal train in the distance.

The sun's rays glittered through the tree line of Pine Mountain that warm October afternoon. John had spent his last day on earth doing what he loved, waxing his 1994 F-150 truck, Ruby Red. He spoke of Ruby with great pride, even after the first 200,000 miles. At first, Julie was skeptical of this woman she had never met. Later, she giggled from the embarrassment of being jealous of a truck.

John and Julie were well known in the little town of Baxter. Having raised four children, three girls and one boy, the family grew quickly with grandchildren. As with life, there were difficult years tempered with the good times. Losing their son to a coal mining accident created a wall between Julie and her beloved husband. Instead of clinging to each other, they seemed to lash out, and at times, they had talked about separation. Many nights John wept alone on the porch, unable to deal with Julie's anger, trying to accept his own crushing emptiness.

Although John acknowledged the pain of losing their only son, Julie kept her bitterness within herself, as if she was afraid to let go, to allow herself to feel a mother's loss. She believed she needed to show strength since her husband shed the tears. Their conflict eased throughout the years, but never resolved. There was no question of their love for each other. That was the tie that bound them together.

John's funeral was simple. Julie abided by his requests for no viewing, no preaching, and no pictures of anyone standing next to his casket. She gave in to his personal favor by placing a bottle of home brew in the casket before the closing. It was a secret between the two of them. The children didn't know their parents sipped from time to time (or so she thought).

After the burial, family and friends gathered at her little house, bringing food and fellowship. Stories were told: some true, some questionable, but all ending in laughter and smiles. The young children played in the yard while the women mingled in the kitchen. The men congregated under a large oak tree near the front gate. The aroma of cigarettes and pipe tobacco permeated the air. Julie sat on the porch in her husband's rocker, simply staring at Ruby Red, not mindful of the grandchildren attempting to attract her attention.

The noise, the chatter, the laughter was muted as she reflected on her memories of the first years with the man she spent most of her life. John taught her how to bait a hook; she taught him how to make biscuits. No major decision was made until both agreed. The marriage was a partnership of deep respect. Their arguments were few, their love passionate. It all changed so quickly when the mine supervisor knocked on their door that fateful evening, with the news of the roof fall at the Black Gold mines.

Their son was the only fatality. The Price family changed that night. Julie's fierce love for her youngest child turned into a determination of blame. After wishing ill will on the mines, mine inspectors, and everyone else connected with their son's death, she questioned her religion. She finally rested her bitterness on the man she loved. It was as if she clung to the pain so that she would not forget her son. As time went on, it simply consumed her.

As the evening sun dipped behind the mountain, the cool air sent all the family and friends away, leaving Julie alone in the home she had shared with John for nearly 50 years. Once inside, she poured a cup of coffee and looked out the kitchen window into the darkness. Her head ached. She felt her anger build to a point of desperation. "Damn it, John Eugene Price! You left me!" Julie cried. "It wasn't supposed to end this way. Your heart was mine! You promised that we would grow old together, that we had many good years ahead. How could you do this to me? To us?"

Suddenly there was a knock on the back door, startling Julie enough that she spilled her coffee on the kitchen counter. She turned on the outside light to see a little boy standing there with a bed pillow under his arm. Julie opened the door. "Raymond, what do you want?"

"I've come to spend the night and keep you company," the young freckle-faced boy answered. "We don't want you to be alone."

"Get on in here. You know better than to be out at night," Julie fussed as she motioned for him to come in. "Does anybody know where you are?"

Raymond entered the dimly lit kitchen. "Yes, ma'am. I was told you'd feel much better if I was to come spend the night."

Julie smiled and shook her head. She was exhausted, and just didn't want to argue with a child. "All right, you can stay."

The boy had a special bond with Julie. He seemed to show up during times of strife and bring a calmness to the old woman.

"Okay, Raymond. Sit down at the kitchen table. I'll cut you a slice of pumpkin pie. I know you need a glass of cold milk to go with it. Bet you can handle that, can't you?"

Raymond showed his toothy smile. "Yes ma'am, I can handle that."

The two sat quietly as she watched the child gobble up the pie. When he was finished, he looked seriously at his friend. "Miss Julie, everything is going to be fine. I just know it. We'll take care of you."

Julie's back stiffened. *How does that boy know it's going to be fine? Nothing is fine. It never will be*, she thought.

"That's really nice of you, Raymond, but I don't need any help. If I ever do, you'll be the first one I call on," Julie answered.

She wished the child had not come. She wanted to curse and scream at the top of her lungs. But now she had a young'un in her house. The Owens had been their neighbors since before Raymond was born. In fact, Julie helped deliver the tiny baby during a heavy snow storm that prevented a trip to the local hospital.

Suddenly it occurred to her that they had not come to John's funeral—but she didn't mention it. She just became more irritated, feeling like she was being snubbed. They had to know about the funeral.

By nine o'clock, Julie pulled the bed covers down for the boy in the spare bedroom. She turned on a night light, just in case he needed to find his way to the bathroom. "Good night, Raymond. Sleep tight, and don't let the bedbugs bite."

"Good night, Miss Julie. We love you," he replied softly.

She returned to the kitchen to wipe the counter and wash the clean plate and empty glass. The quiet was so heavy. No television, no radio, no laughter. The dead emptiness consumed her space. The crushing urge to lash out, to condemn everyone to the fires of hell gripped her body. Her breathing was hard, her pulse rapid and pounding in her head. She hated feeling this way. She felt abandoned, even though her daughters and other family members tried to console her. Nothing was going to fix it. *To have my son back, to have my husband back*, she thought. She was drowning in a pool of self-pity, and she didn't care.

The glass slipped from her soapy hands, hit the side of the sink and shattered. She picked up the larger pieces easily. A tiny sliver cut her finger: not deep, but enough for Julie to break her silence. "Ouch!"

She grabbed a paper towel, tore off a piece, and wrapped it over the cut. She heard shuffling behind her, turned around to see Raymond at the doorway.

"Miss Julie, are you okay?" he asked, rubbing his eyes.

"I'm sorry, Raymond. I didn't mean to wake you. I broke a glass. Got a little cut, that's all. Nothing to worry about. Sorry I hollered."

"It'll be okay. Honest, it will. I'm gonna take care of you." Raymond returned to his bed.

Julie slept soundly that night. Usually she awoke several times during the night, for no reason at all. But this time her body released the exhausting tightness. She welcomed the soft cotton sheets and goose-down pillow. As the morning rain pelted against the window, a clap of thunder caused her not to linger in the bed. She peeked in to see if Raymond was still sleeping. The bed was empty. Walking into the living room, she found the boy curled up on the couch, looking at an old photo album that had been left on the coffee table.

"Morning, Miss Julie."

"Good morning, Raymond. Have you been up long?"

"Just a little while. I tried to be quiet, but that storm wasn't gonna let me sleep," he said.

"Are you hungry?"

"Miss Julie, you know I'm always hungry."

"I'll fix us a breakfast, but first I gotta have my coffee."

Raymond nodded.

Julie brewed a pot of coffee and got two cups out of the cabinet, out of habit. She turned, then carefully placed John's favorite cup back on the shelf. Her hands trembled. Again, she wished that child would just leave.

The aroma of fried bacon, scrambled eggs, and buttered toast soon filled the kitchen. "Raymond!" she yelled. ""Breakfast is ready. Come and get it."

Julie sat across from the boy, as he ate a meal fit for a king. John always told her that. "Honey, don't you think you need to call your mother?"

"No ma'am. Everything's just fine. I promise it is."

Julie went over to the kitchen phone on the wall. "Well, I just think I'll give her a call and let her know you are fine." She picked up the phone. No dial tone. "Gee, honey, the phone's dead. It must be really storming down the road."

Raymond grinned. "Don't worry. Mom and Dad know where I am."

The rain stopped after breakfast. The sun moved from behind the clouds, a rainbow of brilliant colors spanned the sky. They went out on the porch to admire God's handiwork. Julie took her rightful place in John's damp rocker. Raymond grabbed a small footstool to sit next to her. Raindrops glistened against the grass. The colors of the leaves created exquisite bouquets. The air was cleansed and fresh. She wondered if John could see all this beauty.

"Look Miss Julie!" Raymond shouted, pointing to the birdfeeder in the yard. "Look! It's a red cardinal."

"I see it, child. It's beautiful."

"But Miss Julie, don't you know that if you see a red cardinal, it's really someone who has died is coming back to say hello? Honest. My Mama told me."

Julie shook her head. "Oh, I don't know about that."

Raymond took her hand. "It's true. You have to believe, Miss Julie."

There was something in the way Raymond spoke that brought Julie a peace within her heart. "I'll think about that, but I'm making no promises."

An hour later, Raymond told her he was going to go on home. He thought she would be all right for a while. Julie agreed. He stood on the porch with his pillow under his arm. "Thank you, Miss Julie, for having me. If you ever need anything, anything at all, I'll come running."

"I'm really glad you came, Raymond. Thank you. You have a good heart, young man."

"I sure did enjoy looking at that album of old pictures. Mr. John loved you mighty strong. You ought to look at those pictures when you have a chance. It might make you happy," he said softly. "Bye for now."

She watched him as he walked down the lane. She loved that boy even when he pestered her. She thought he was an old soul in a child's body. As she walked through the living room, she glanced over at the tattered album still on the coffee table. *Maybe I'll look at it tonight*, she thought.

"No," she said aloud. "What else have I got to do with my time? I'll just look at the pictures now."

Julie sat on the couch and opened the album to the first page. She turned each page full with decades of memories, of her parents and other relatives, her children, and her John. In the folds of the last page, she found a letter addressed to her. The envelope was recent, the handwriting was definitely John's, and it was sealed. Her hands trembled as she opened it.

> Dear Julie,
>
> My time on this earth is over. We had some good times, some bad, and a few hard times. But I want you to know I have always loved you. When I'm gone, don't mourn for me because I will watch over you and protect you the best I can, just as I tried to do all our lives together. Our son waits for me, and I know someday we will all be together. Take care of yourself, and leave any regrets behind. And for heaven sakes, be happy.
>
> Your Loving Husband,
> John

The holler filled with Julie's burst of tears. So much pain! She slid off the couch onto the floor holding the letter to her bosom. *When did he write this? There were lots of people looking at that album after the funeral. No one said a word about a letter. How did it get in this album?* She rocked her body back and forth on the floor. She lay there, closed her eyes, and sobbed until exhausted.

The next time Julie opened her eyes, it was late afternoon. She checked the phone for a dial tone. It was working. She called the Owens residence to thank them for sending Raymond over, and to ask the boy if he saw that envelope in the album earlier. Cheryl Owens answered the phone.

"Cheryl, I just want to thank you so very much for sending Raymond over here to stay last night. That was very thoughtful of you. He is such a fine young man," Julie said. "I think…"

"No!" Cheryl interrupted loudly. "No, Julie, that can't be. You're wrong."

"What do you mean, Honey?"

"You don't know. You really don't know! Oh, God!" Cheryl cried.

"What?"

"Our baby boy passed away yesterday. He'd been in the hospital with pneumonia and took a turn for the worse. Raymond died in my arms. He couldn't have been at your house. That's why we weren't at John's funeral."

"Oh, Cheryl, I am so sorry. I don't know what to say. Please forgive me. I'll talk to you later," Julie said and hung up the phone.

She sat on the porch in the rocker for hours, trying to make sense of the past few days. It was damp. It was cold. She didn't care.

"John, I guess I thought that lashing out from losing our son was a way of surviving. You tried so hard to understand me, and I pushed you away. I am so terribly sorry. I have loved you, I love you now, and I will always love you. Thank you for all the wonderful years we had together. I know I am one stubborn woman. It took the spirit of a child to calm my soul. It took your beautiful letter to bring me peace. For that I thank you. My life is not the same, nor should it be. I will be okay."

Through her tears, she talked to John aloud as if he was beside her. Maybe he was.

The End

Last One to Leave

Sharyn Martin

"**L**et's go sit over here on the bench," she said. The last strains of "Amazing Grace" faded away, and the clouds covered the faint winter sun. The trees looked like bony fingers reaching toward heaven, and the mute, white stones gave their testimony of the souls gone on...either to heaven or hell. They all looked the same from the bench.

Mama and I had just attended a graveside service for another one of her friends. This time it was Nola Larkin. She and Mama had been in the same Sunday School class, until Nola had gotten so ill.

"Nola was a good woman. One of the best quilters I've ever seen. Her work could be recognized anywhere. Did you know she never married? She stayed on the home place and took care of her parents 'til they died, then sold off some land and traveled to Europe every summer for years. I've still got postcards from Paris and London and all those places. Nola never was afraid to fly."

Pine Ridge looked down on us, stark in the winter sky. "I don't guess you remember your granddaddy talking about the Edwards family. Lucy and Ben had one daughter named Caroline, and she loved the boy who helped Ben with the farm. One evening, they came in and announced they were getting married. They'd been sneaking around for months, and Lucy never did know. Ben suspected something, but never said anything. At least, that's what your granddaddy told me. Well, Lucy threw a fit. She said they never would marry, and she'd see to it. She lived to regret that statement. They left that night—bitter cold it was, too—and went to the preacher over in Poor Valley. He married them that night, and they went to a cabin back up at the edge of Pine Ridge. This cabin was just a shelter for the farm workers, and it had no windows or doors. Caroline's daddy knew the two had been meeting there, and he figured that's where they'd go. He got some blankets from Caroline's room and started out the front door, but Lucy stopped him. 'You'll never step foot in here again if you help that girl ruin her life like she's ruined mine.' Ben left the next morning with some supplies, taking them to Caroline at the cabin. He walked in and there was the young couple, huddled together in the corner of the one room, frozen to death. Lucy still refused to accept the fact that Caroline had disobeyed and married someone so beneath her (or so she thought), and the two were buried over there by the fence in an unmarked grave. Ben never came back here after the burial, and Lucy is buried with her parents in the family plot."

Mama patted her navy-blue hat: the one she called her "funeral hat." She only owned two; the other one was red, and Mama never would wear red to a funeral. It was a scandalous color. Her daddy never would let his daughters wear red, and Mama never owned a red dress 'til after she was married.

"Over there is where they buried Fern. I can remember when she moved here. We were both just young, and her boy was a year older than you. We used to sit out in the yard and break beans while you all played under the trees. She had a hard life up 'til Arthur died. He was the meanest man I ever knew. I remember one time he hit her so hard, it left a bruise on her face for over two weeks. I was the only one she told, and she stayed out of church for at least a month. She was afraid somebody would ask her about it, and she wanted it to be all gone before she came back. I used to beg her to leave that man, but she always said she didn't have any place else to go. She used to raise chickens and sell the eggs down at the store. Arthur got up one morning and the chickens had messed all over that old car he left out all the time. When Fern looked out the window, all the chickens were scattered around the yard. Arthur had wrung their necks. She came over here and I went back with her. We picked chickens all morning and canned them that afternoon. She couldn't afford not to use them, but she cried all the time we were working. She did have a few good years before she died, but I always felt so sorry for her. She sure had a lot of misery in her life."

I looked around the cemetery. Mama always said it was the fastest growing subdivision in the valley. It seemed like every time we drove by we saw a new grave or a tent from the funeral home. We sat quietly and watched the squirrels playing, listening to their chatter. Each of us had our own thoughts: Mama probably thinking about the dead, and me wondering about the living.

"That little bitty rock over there was where Etta Grace buried her second baby. Everybody around here always thought he was the first child, but I know different. Etta Grace and me went back a long ways. I've been here most of my life, and Etta Grace was my friend before we moved over here. She got mixed up with a boy who worked with the carnival, and I guess you know what happened. Etta Grace's parents were so strict, and her having a baby without being married was the worst thing they could imagine. One night, I remember it was raining, her little sister came up the lane to our house and knocked on my bedroom window. I opened the window, and Louise was crying and begging me to come with her to the house. She said the baby was coming too early and Etta Grace was in terrible pain, but wouldn't let Louise tell her mother. When we got there, Etta Grace was lying on the bed, blood everywhere, and a small bundle was on the floor beside the bed. I was scared half to death, but we gathered up everything, cleaned Etta Grace, and left her there while we went out to the orchard. We buried that little thing in the orchard and never told a soul. I'm telling you now, 'cause there's nobody left who'd care. Etta Grace was weak and sick for at least a month, but she never mentioned the baby again, and her parents acted like it had never existed. She never did tell them what had happened. That was one of the hardest things I've ever done in my life, but I never did feel like it was wrong. That baby needed a decent burial, and we gave it one in the prettiest place you ever saw. We had him all wrapped up in a lace curtain—that was the best we could do—and put him in a box. Every spring that orchard bloomed out so pretty, and I always thought what a beautiful place it was to be in forever. Etta Grace finally met a man in town who had been widowed and left with two children. She married him and had one baby that died, then had a little girl. How she doted on that child! Etta Grace has been gone now for several years, but I still miss her. I used to take the bus to town and visit with her and stay all day. We would have the best time."

"Mama, do you want to go back to the car? It's getting a little cool for you out here."

"Let's wait a little while. I'll be alright. See that big stone over there? The one that looks like an open gate? That's where the Bensons are buried. They were fine people, and pretty well off. Their daughter went completely crazy one afternoon and shot them both. They had a big farm down on the river. She had been out to the barn all day, and just came in that evening and started shooting. She shot her daddy as soon as she came in the house, and then went upstairs and shot her mother. They said her mother had been changing the sheets on the bed, and just fell across them like she was asleep. Nobody ever did know what happened or why, but the courts sent her off to a mental hospital. As far as I know, she's still there."

"Eva Bell is buried down there off to the right. When I was just a little girl, I remember her coming to the house pretty often. She always brought something to sell. Sometimes it was a dress, and one time a clock that she said had belonged to her mother. We never did have any extra money to help her, but I remember Mama and Daddy talking when I wasn't supposed to hear. Eva Bell used the money she got from selling all her stuff to buy Paregoric. She was addicted to it and would go buy it at the drugstore in town. There wasn't anybody in town who'd pay for a plot in the cemetery there, so the funeral home asked if she could be buried here. The folks who run the place agreed, and she does have a little marble footstone."

"Miss Rebecca Smith is over there, with the little stone that has the angel on top. She used to make sure everybody had something to eat that needed it, or something warm to wear in the winter. I remember one time Mildred Davis called her over to their house. Mildred was dying with lung cancer, and wanted to know if Miss Rebecca would get her a dress to be laid out in. Miss Rebecca took the bus from the main road into town and went to the finest store on Broad Street. She got Mildred a beautiful white and pink dress and took it to her. Mildred cried when she saw that dress, and asked Miss Rebecca to hang it on the door where she could look at it. It wasn't too long after that Mildred died. She's buried toward the back of the cemetery. I think of Mildred and Miss Rebecca a lot. I don't guess any of the Davis people ever paid Miss Rebecca for that dress, but I'm sure she didn't mind. She was just that kind of person, always taking care of somebody else."

I glanced over at her; Mama looked so tiny and delicate, but she was one of the toughest people I ever knew. I had heard all the stories she had told me this afternoon, but it made her feel better to tell them again. All these people here were my extended family, and there are no people left for Mama to talk to that remember life as it had been so many years earlier.

"We've had a lot of sorrow in this community, but a lot of good times, too. I miss all my friends. I've had a better life than most of them. I'll be eighty-seven this year, and that's older than any of them lived to be. I guess we can go now. We're the last to leave."

The End

My Decision

Linda Hudson Hoagland

"Before the end of this day, I will make my decision," I told my coworker.

"You can't be serious," she responded, in a voice dripping with sarcasm.

"I've never been more serious about anything in my life," I said, a smile spreading across my face.

"I'm so glad you are joking," Nancy said, with a matching smile.

"I'm not joking. I'm going to do it," I added in a stronger tone.

"Ellen, no, please don't. He will make your life a living hell. You know that, don't you?"

"Mary, someone has got to do it. For your information only, until I tell personnel, I already have another job. I'm sure they will give me nothing but trouble when I give them my two-week notice. You know how they are. They always want to punish the person leaving. If it gets to be unbearable, I won't work the two weeks," I explained.

"Where are you going to work?" asked Mary.

"I'm going to work for Glen at Royalton Steel," I said with a conspiratorial grin.

"More money?" Mary asked.

"Of course," I answered.

"When are you leaving?" asked Mary.

"After I have my little talk with the Vice President," I said in a low whisper.

"Ellen, are you sure you want to do that?" asked a concerned Mary.

"Mary, you know how Benny operates," I said.

"Everybody knows," whispered Mary.

"Everybody except Mr. Jameson. If he knew what was going on, he would do something about it," I said softly.

"Are you sure, Ellen?"

"No, not really—but I've got to tell someone I think might do something about it," I explained.

"And you think that someone is Mr. Jameson?" asked Mary.

"Who else is there to tell?" I asked.

"You've got a point," said Mary with a long sigh.

"I have a four o'clock appointment with Mr. Jameson, so I will talk to him just before I go home for the day. Wish me luck, Mary."

"No, Ellen, I don't want to wish you luck, because I don't want you to go. You will have to go if you tell on Benny."

"Lunch is over. We have to get back," I said, urging her to get a move on.

"But I have so many questions to ask you," said a frustrated Mary.

"They will have to wait," I said.

I was soon back at my desk doing a job I absolutely hated, because Benny decided I should do credit and collections.

Because I had been Glen's administrative assistant and Benny got Glen fired, he didn't want me anywhere near his sales staff. Eventually, I would be able to fulfill a promise I made to myself and Glen; Benny was going to play a big part in that promise.

Benny thought moving me to credit and collections would keep me away from his young, pretty, inside sales trainees. Being an old lady in her early 30s with two little boys in tow, I just didn't fit his mold of promotable material.

I had already made the necessary collection calls for the day. The customers I had to call were always the same ones; most of them were barely keeping their companies running from job to job, and no amount of talk from me was going to make them pay any faster. The only time I would get any real action from a delinquent customer was when I cut off the credit. Most of the time, I had only to make the threat and suddenly a check would appear. I didn't like doing that. I don't like to be threatened, and I don't like to threaten anyone else. But it was my job, and I had to do it.

I shuffled papers for the rest of the afternoon. I tried to make myself look busy, even though I was absolutely bored to tears. I was not going to miss this job, not even a little bit.

The longer I thought about what I was going to tell Mr. Jameson, the more nervous I became. This waiting and worrying was for the birds. Clock watching made time pass much slower. I knew that for a fact. An hour could drag on forever.

At 3:45 PM, I made my way to the ladies' room to check the condition of my short hair and powder my always shiny nose. I had already locked up my desk and turned off the typewriter and calculator so I could leave the building straight from Mr. Jameson's office. His secretary, Nancy, told me she would sign my time card if I didn't get to punch out on time.

Nancy tried her level best to pry the information out of me about why I wanted to talk to Mr. Jameson when I scheduled the appointment. I knew she would try again when I appeared in her office, which was just outside of Mr. Jameson's office. Anyone who wanted to exchange words with Mr. Jameson had to speak with Nancy first.

I took a deep breath and walked out of the ladies' room, headed straight into an unknown future.

"Hey, Nancy. I'm here for my appointment with Mr. Jameson," I said. I spoke through a big fake smile.

"Just have a seat, Ellen. As soon as he hangs up the telephone I will send you in. Now, what was the reason for the meeting?" Nancy asked.

"I just need to talk with Mr. Jameson," I answered curtly.

"Does he know what it's about?" she continued.

"No, I don't think so," I responded, trying to spit out as few words as possible.

"Usually he tells me what file he needs me to pull. If you tell me the topic of your discussion, I'll see if I can find the necessary file," Nancy probed.

"You won't need to do that, Nancy. Nothing is on paper, and I doubt that it ever will be," I replied sharply, hoping she would finally get the message that I was not going to tell her anything.

"It's a big secret, is it?" Nancy asked, a smirk appearing on her lips.

"For the moment," I said. I looked toward Mr. Jameson's office door.

Nancy glanced at the telephone, seeing that none of the lines were shining brightly.

"You can go in now, Ellen."

"Thank you, Nancy," I said with a smile that was purely fake.

"Ellen, what can I do for you? You sounded so mysterious when you asked for an appointment," said Mr. Jameson as I entered his office.

"Mr. Jameson, as you know I was Glen's right arm when he worked here, and I was very proud of that. When he was fired and replaced by Benny, of course I was unhappy, but I didn't think I would be punished for having performed my job to the best of my ability," I said slowly building up speed to get to the rest of the revelation.

"You were and are an excellent employee, and you are not being punished," interrupted Robert Jameson.

"Yes sir, I am. I was placed in a job I absolutely hate, by a man who knew I did not want to do credit and collections," I explained.

"I was told differently," Jameson replied.

"Then you were told a lie," I said, looking straight into his eyes.

"We can rectify that, Ellen."

"No sir, you can't. I haven't finished speaking my piece yet. May I continue?" I said.

"Yes."

"The first moment I laid eyes on Benny, I knew what he was going to do. I actually told Glen that he had hired his replacement as soon as I was able to get him away from the crowd of well-wishers gathered around Benny. That doesn't matter anymore. What matters is that in order to be promoted to a more lucrative inside sales job, I am required to have sex with Benny. I refuse to do that, Mr. Jameson."

For a moment, Robert Jameson was speechless. He sat up straighter in his chair and looked at me like a disbelieving father.

"Can you prove what you are saying? Did he approach you?" he snapped.

"No, I wouldn't ask for the job because of the requirement. But you might want to ask your former secretary, Myra, and some of the new trainees, who allow him to treat them like lap dogs," I said.

"Why would I ask them about sexual harassment claims if you can't prove them?" he asked.

"I'd think you might want to avoid the potential lawsuit. I did overhear a conversation when I was in a stall in the ladies' room. I don't believe Myra and Nancy knew I was there listening. It was not intentional, but I did hear the conversation. I will try to repeat it word for word."

"Nancy said, 'Myra, do you like working for Benny?'

"'Sure, he is really nice to us. We each get a night with him all to ourselves,' answered Myra.

"'What are you talking about, Myra?'

"'Tuesday is my night. I get him all night long. I get to do whatever I want with him, and he loves every minute of it.'

"'What about his wife?' asked Nancy.

"'She gets him all weekend. The other girls have their days, too,' said Myra.

"'If I want an inside sales job, would Benny give me one?' asked Nancy.

"'I'm sure he would. He still has a day left during the week,' said Myra.

"'I would have to sleep with Benny every week? asked Nancy.

"'Yes, that's required. You don't mind, do you?' asked Myra.

"Nancy replied, 'No, for a possible ten thousand dollars a year raise, I think I can do it.'"

"That was the end of their conversation, because I flushed the toilet," I said.

"Did they see you?" Jameson asked.

"No, but I'm sure when they realized someone was in the stall they probably could tell who it was from squatting down to look at my feet," I said with a smile.

"Ellen, this should not be happening," he said apologetically.

"Yes sir, I know. That is why I'm telling you, so you can do something about it," I said. I made my voice as firm as I could, almost forceful.

"I will check into this," he said, flustered.

"One more thing, Mr. Jameson. I want to give you my two-week notice," I said.

Again, he looked at me, stunned, obviously at a loss for words.

"Goodnight, Mr. Jameson," I said. I walked out of his office passing Nancy's empty desk. It was beyond quitting time, and she was gone for the day.

Bright and early the next morning, Benny was standing in front of me looking all bent out of shape.

"What were you talking to Mr. Jameson about?" he demanded.

"That's between Mr. Jameson and me, Benny. I don't have to tell you," I replied slowly and softly so the looky-loos wouldn't understand what I was saying.

"Were you complaining about your job?" he demanded.

"Yes, among other things," I answered smugly.

"What other things?" he shouted.

"That's none of your business, Benny," I shouted back at him.

"You're fired!"

"You can't fire me, Benny!"

"Why not?" he sputtered.

"Why don't you ask Mr. Jameson?"

"I will do just that. Pack up your belongings and get out of here!" he snapped.

"No. Go talk to Mr. Jameson. I will not leave until you talk with him," I said with a broad smile.

Benny stomped from my desk and ran up the steps to the second floor.

I stood up slowly, grabbed my handbag, and walked to the ladies' room. I hid in there in a stall for what seemed to be an hour.

"Ellen, please report to Mr. Jameson's office," screeched the intercom system throughout the building.

I tensed up. It was really going to hit the fan now.

Nancy was not at her desk, so I knocked on Mr. Jameson's door.

"Come in, Ellen," he said loudly.

I opened the door; no one was in there except Mr. Jameson.

"Ellen, would you reconsider your decision about leaving the company?" he asked pleasantly.

"No sir."

"If I told you Benny is no longer an employee, would you stay?" he asked.

"No sir, I think it's too late for that."

"Things will be different, thanks to you," he explained.

"I hope so, sir, but people have long memories. My presence here will be a reminder. Thank you for the offer. I do appreciate it," I said sincerely.

I walked out of his office and away from the company, never to return.

I was soon working with Glen again, and loving every minute of it. Strangely enough, I had the blessing of his wonderful wife. Glen was not my direct supervisor. Actually, I worked for his boss.

The atmosphere was much more pleasant, and sex with my supervisor was not a prerequisite.

"Ellen, I ran into Benny yesterday," said a smiling Glen.

"Did he have anything interesting to say?" I asked.

"He told me he no longer works at Wellington-Lewis. Did you know that?" Glen asked.

"Yes sir, I did. What else did he have to say?"

"He said he had never in his life run into anyone as loyal as you are to me. He also said that I should watch you closely, and never make an enemy out of you. Do you know what he is talking about?" asked Glen.

I smiled and whispered, "I got him, Glen. I told you I would."

The End

Patchwork Hearts

Willie E. Dalton

Growing up, I always wanted the same kind of life my parents had. Their love for one another was like a river—to an observer it looked calm, and dare I say it, boring. But just underneath the surface, it was powerful, with a current strong enough to carry them over and around every rock and obstacle they encountered. Together, they ran their farm, raised five children, and had enough love for everyone.

I was a bit of an odd child, but my parents never treated me as such. I spent a lot of time with the animals on the farm, and a lot of time with Mom in the kitchen. Cooking for her family was her favorite thing to do. I found it peaceful to watch her work. I'd sit and talk with her while she pitted cherries and rolled out dough, stealing little tastes here and there. My brothers and sisters always seemed to be doing something else. I was never outgoing enough to keep up with them. It didn't bother me though; I always spent my time exactly where I wanted.

One day, when I was about nine or ten, I noticed oddly-shaped fuzzy colors on Mom's chest. At first, I thought she had spilled something on her shirt. When I asked her about it, she had no idea what I was talking about. She repeatedly looked down at her blouse, trying to dust off whatever she thought I was seeing. I thought maybe something was wrong with my eyes and told her never mind.

Throughout the day, my brothers and sisters wandered through the house; I saw nothing strange on them. But when Dad came in, I was shocked to see the same fuzzy colors on his chest, exactly the same as Mom's. I didn't speak of my new-found ability to anyone. For weeks, I just watched everyone around me. The colors never faded. They only grew brighter and more clearly defined. Over time, I began to see colors and patterns on the chests of other people. It was years later that I realized I was seeing their hearts: I was seeing love.

My 17-year-old sister had been dating a boy for several months when I noticed new colors starting to appear on her chest, just over her heart. Not long after, whenever her boyfriend came by, I saw the same colors and pattern forming on his heart as well. I observed their relationship quietly, and watched as their colors gradually became brighter. After several months of mutual adoration, they began to argue. As the arguments grew, the colors over their hearts became dull and muted. Eventually, they parted ways. Later, as she began to fall in love again, new colors began to form in another place on her heart. After a time, I learned that every love and loss left a mark on a person's heart.

One day, I saw the fuzzy hues of pink and violet forming on the chest of my best guy friend, Doug. I knew he was falling in love with me. I hesitated to let our love grow, because I had made it known to him I wanted to stay close to where I grew up. I wanted to run my own farm, as my parents had done. Doug, on the other hand, had always dreamed of being a businessman in a city far away from the Appalachian Mountains we called home. Despite our concerns, our love deepened. When he proposed, he assured me he would be happy on a farm as long as he was with me. And for a while, he was.

Getting started in our own farm life was not easy. It seemed as though everything we tried to do was an uphill battle. Getting a loan for the farm was a nearly insurmountable feat. Restoring the old farmhouse and working the land itself was unending. Bills piled up faster than the crops could grow, but I stayed optimistic. I was so sure our love would see us through this rough patch of life, and once we were through it, happiness was just around the corner.

Even though times were hard, we still loved each other. Through that love, we had two daughters who brought me joy like I had never known. Along with joy, though, children bring responsibility—and a need for steady income. Doug worked hard on the farm. Day after day, from daylight to darkness, he worked his fingers to the bone—sometimes almost literally. I wanted us to run the farm as partners, like my parents had. But anytime I tried to help him in the fields or barn, he sent me back to the house, saying that I wasn't cut out for that work. I appreciated the concern, but I knew I wasn't as fragile as he believed. Doug wanted my focus to be the children and the house. I acquiesced.

It didn't happen overnight. It happened over years; it happened so slowly I was able to steady myself for its coming. I watched the colors of his love for me slowly fade as he began to resent me. I had my contentment in our daughters, but he was always out on the farm. His little time with us was spent hurriedly gulping down meals or falling asleep in his chair before bed. This was never the life he wanted. Maybe I should have tried harder to make him love me again, but I didn't know how. Maybe I should have told him to leave sooner, but I thought I couldn't make it without him. And so, I watched his love for me die—and I let it, until one day our colors were just a faded memory.

I wasn't surprised when one morning I woke up in an empty bed. He was often out and gone when I got up in the mornings, but this morning something was different. I started the coffee pot and looked in on the girls; they were already up, getting ready for school.

"Have you all seen your dad?" I asked.

They told me he had come in their room and kissed them on the head before daylight. It was what had woken them.

A short time later, a knock at the door confirmed my suspicion. It was Hal, one of our farm hands. He was wondering if Doug was sick, since he hadn't made it outside yet. Twelve years of living here, and Doug had only missed a day or two.

I did my best to choke back my tears, but one escaped and rolled down my cheek. I was quiet for a minute as I thought about what to say, what to do. I straightened my spine and pulled back my shoulders, then did the only thing I could do.

"Hal," I said, "He's not here, and I don't think he's coming back. I need you to show me how to run the farm."

His eyes widened with surprise, and he started to apologize. I put my hand up and shook my head.

"I'll be fine," I said, as the last tear I would shed over my husband slipped down my cheek.

The first two weeks were the hardest. My body wasn't used to that kind of work, and it ached in ways I didn't think possible. My hands were calloused and bloody, my neck sunburnt, and my back was in knots, but I made it through.

When the girls weren't in school, they usually came outside to play and talk with me or Hal while we worked. Whenever they asked about their dad, I just told them he was gone and they never asked anything more. They were old enough to understand.

One evening, I realized they hadn't been outside that day to visit. I had heard them giggling and making a racket in the house, so I knew they were fine; it was just odd they hadn't been out. I finished up my work and went inside. To my astonishment, the house was clean and dinner was on the table.

My girls smiled and fixed me a plate. "We thought if you were having to do Dad's job, we should do yours."

I stood there staring at my beautiful daughters and cried. I wasn't missing a husband; I wasn't missing anything.

One morning a couple of months later, I finally received the papers. I stood by the tractor while I read them. He let me have the farm, house, and everything that went with it. The amount of child support he agreed to was less than I deserved but I'd be happy to get it, so I signed just to be finished with the whole thing. I was hurt and angry. So much was left unsaid, but it was too late now.

It was once again the time of year to plant the flower bulbs of lilies and tulips for the greenhouse that opened in the spring. This had been the one part of the garden I had tended to every year. This year, I was having trouble digging the holes for the bulbs. The ground seemed even more rocky and hard than usual. Nearly exhausted after digging three holes, I still had rows and rows to go. I stopped to wipe the sweat from my brow and heard Hal's voice behind me.

"You're fighting the earth; you have to work with it," he said.

He knelt down beside me and took my tools. He easily dug hole after hole for me. I followed along behind him, dropping in the bulbs.

"You have to think about working *with* the elements. The earth, rain, and sun, they all nourish the things we plant and harvest. If you fight against the elements, like you have some kind of control, they'll fight back," he laughed.

That was the first moment I really looked at Hal. I had known him for at least ten years, but now... Instead of a farm hand, I saw something else. Every morning since Doug left, Hal had shown up at my door, coffee in hand, to show me how to run this place. I had made his days longer and his work harder, but he never once complained.

After we finished planting the flower bulbs, I walked over and hugged him. He was caught by surprise, to say the least. He half laughed, but hugged me back.

"Thank you," I said. I kept my arms tight around his neck.

"Why, you're welcome. You would've gotten the hang of all this eventually," he said.

"Maybe, but you have made it so much easier for me and the girls."

"You and your girls are my favorite people," he said.

Slowly, I began to fall in love with the farm again. The joy I'd felt as a child on my parents' farm was returning. Once I knew how everything was supposed to run and the money started slowly coming in, I relaxed. The girls pitched in wherever they could before school, and they came to love living there, just like I did.

I woke up every morning and had my coffee on the porch with Hal, and we'd talk about the things we needed to do for the day. Sometimes we'd just sit quietly and breathe in the fresh, spicy scent of the garden. If you were up early enough, you could watch a light mist hovering over the grass as the sun rose up behind the barn. There was a stillness and magic to our farm that I never tired of experiencing.

One morning as Hal sat across from me, I saw his heart for the first time. Maybe it was just the first time I truly looked. There were several faded colors and patterns of love in his past, and a new one growing.

I felt a heat in my own chest spreading up to my face at the idea it could be me he was falling in love with. But I wasn't sure it was about me, and I didn't know how to ask. So, I did the last thing I would expect myself to do: I told Hal about what I could see. I told him about it all, from the very beginning. From being in the kitchen with Mom, seeing the progression of my brothers' and sisters' relationships, to watching my husband's love for me die. And I told him how every love leaves its mark on the heart. When I was finished, he sat thoughtfully for a minute and then laughed.

"If every love leaves a mark, my heart probably looks like a patchwork quilt," He said. There was no judgement, no disbelief; he just sat and sipped his coffee.

I reached over and took his hand, my fingers curling around his. He nodded without ever looking right at me, and said, "You can see it, can't you?" He smiled.

I moved in a little closer to him and laid my head on his shoulder. "I love you, too."

The next spring, we were married by the flower garden. All the flowers he had helped me plant were in full bloom. Hal and I grew a love on that farm that was as strong as Mom and Dads'. He loved my girls like his own. And oh, how they loved him! In time, we had a son, and then our family was complete. Our patchwork hearts were complete: painful scraps of memories stitched together with faith and hope, then finished with love.

The End

Rainbow Bright

Charlotte H. Deskins

Louise Stiltner watched as the doors of the high school opened and the student body of Coaltown High School, home of the Coaltown Cougars, came spilling out. A crowd of cheerleaders, dressed in the school's colors of maroon and gold, tumbled down the steps. Among them was Misty Dawn Stiltner—the prettiest one, in Louise's humble opinion. The fact that "Midi," as her friends called her, was Louise's granddaughter had absolutely nothing to do with her assessment. Or not much, anyhow.

Louise took one final drag off her Salem Light and crushed the butt out in Rainbow Bright's ash tray. She rolled down the window and yelled, "Misty! Hey, Miss—over here!"

Louise's heart sank a little as the tall blonde girl dramatically rolled her eyes at the boy standing next to her. She whispered something in his ear, gave him a quick kiss, and sauntered slowly over. "Mommaw, what are you doing here? I told you I was gonna ride home with Topher on his bike today."

"Like I would let any self-respecting granddaughter of mine fly around town on that crotch rocket of his! Especially in that short skirt!"

"Well, not to worry. I'm covering all the important parts!" Misty Dawn turned and gave a little can-can type flip, revealing tiny maroon shorts underneath her uniform. ""And for your information, his bike is not a crotch rocket! It's a Honda CB1000R." She gave her boyfriend a farewell wave and watched as he ambled toward his motorcycle.

Now it was Louise's turn to roll her eyes. But at least Misty didn't look all high and mighty anymore. She had been distant with Louise ever since she started going around with that Christopher Crigger. He seemed like a nice enough boy, but Louise just knew he had a wild streak in him. The women in her family were always drawn to the no good, good-looking ones. She had first-hand knowledge about that sort of thing.

Reaching over, Louise popped open the passenger side door. Rainbow groaned and squeaked. Sometimes she had a tendency to stick just a little. Misty plopped herself down and pulled down the vanity mirror to look herself over. "And in my day, boys named Christopher got called Chris, not Topher. Topher sounds like something the cat dragged in, and couldn't be bothered to kill!" Louise started the car and pulled away from the curb.

"Your day was a *long* time ago!" Misty shot back, but her blue eyes twinkled in jest. The two of them bickered constantly, but neither could stay mad for long.

Louise looked herself over in the rearview mirror. Truer words were never spoken. She looked like a washed out, heavier version of her granddaughter. Her eye bags were carrying their own sets of luggage these days, and her jawline was a map to a place she wouldn't want to visit for five minutes—let alone live in. She needed to lose 15—no, make that 20—all right, 25 pounds. She sighed. When had she stopped caring about herself?

"I thought you and I would go shopping for prom dresses today." Louise tried to keep the tremor out of her voice.

Misty grinned, showing her perfect teeth. Louise had worked long and hard to provide braces for those teeth. "Are you sure you want to let me go? With the family curse and all."

Louise felt a shiver down her back. "I admit, I have my reservations. But I don't want you to miss your prom!"

Louise drifted back to her own prom, back in 1979. Back to the night the curse began.

She had come down the stairs wearing her peasant-style evening gown, sea green eye shadow, and lipstick to meet her frowning mother. ""Where do you think you're going, looking like that?" Her mother demanded.

"It's just a little makeup, Mama," Louise pleaded. "Just for this special occasion. I want to look nice."

"You look like a whore," her mother spat. "I hate to think what Sister Maggie and Brother Richard would think, if they saw you like that."

"Oh, for Pete's sake, Janice," her father said. "Can't you leave the church out of it for one night?!" Louise shot her father a grateful look.

Her mother's eyes hardened. She said no more. Louise paced anxiously until her steady boyfriend, Rigger Bradshaw, showed up in his old hot rod station wagon, wearing a powder blue tux, and blew the horn for her to come out. As she picked up her white yarn shawl, her mother grabbed her by the arm and whispered in her ear. "You just watch and see! God will curse you for your sinful ways! Remember that!" Louise slammed the door with shaking hands.

Her mother turned out to be right. It wasn't how she looked that ruined her, but what happened after. She didn't even know why she did it. Maybe just to get back at her mother, to rebel. Maybe because she was afraid she was losing Rigger, and she wanted him to stay close to her. After the dance, she and Rigger went on out to the slate dump and she did things she had never done before. She cried when it was over. She felt as if she had lost herself and would never be the same.

One month later, she missed her period. In tears, she called Rigger. He seemed tickled to death at first, and talked about getting married. But as soon as graduation was over, he and his garage band left town. She heard from him a few times, mostly funny postcards—then nothing. A silence settled over her, and panic followed closely. She started to feel like she couldn't breathe; it was then she realized that in a very real way, her life was over.

In the end, her folks took it better than expected. They certainly weren't happy, but they weren't going to throw her out of the house. Her mother wailed on and on about how she couldn't show her face in church. Until her dying day, she never forgave Louise. Her daddy stood by her. He must have taken a lot of abuse from the men he worked with down at the mine, but he never took it out on Louise.

One evening she was standing at the kitchen sink washing the dishes, eight months along and ready to pop. She looked around and there stood Daddy in the hallway, just looking at her. He had a little smile on his face. "What's so funny?" she asked. He was quiet for a minute. "I was just thinking how much you look like my own Ma standing there." He said.

Louise was taken aback. "She must have looked a sorry sight," she sighed, running her hands over her belly. Her dad walked over and kissed the top of her head. "She was a strong, beautiful woman," he said. "And so is her granddaughter."

Louise forgot about the curse. She didn't think of it again for a long time. She found a job, working at the local hospital in the clerical and billing department. She worked until her baby, a little girl she named Angel, was born. After that, she came right back to her job. Her daddy and his buddies built her a little house out back of where her parents lived. It was basic, but nice enough for her and Angel. Louise was expected to keep it clean and pay all her utilities on time, which she did. In fact, she became so efficient and regimented it was scary. She was in charge of her life and her future.

Except she wasn't. Angel, by her very existence, saw to that.

From the start, she was the exact opposite of her namesake. She was independent, with a stubborn steak wide enough to drive a tractor through. And she had a darkness in her.

She shaved off all her dolls' hair and drew tattoos on them. She shredded the pretty flowered wallpaper Louise spent hours lovingly applying to the walls, and rolled black and purple paint on its place. She refused to do her chores or obey any curfews. Although the teachers said she was smart, she went out of her way to get failing grades. Angel, it seemed did not fit into their little coal mining town. She did not fit in anywhere.

Privately, Louise wondered how she had come to give birth to such a strange child so unlike herself. Was it the influence of Rigger's blood? His whole family was always a little bit crazy. At times like this, she thought once again of her mother's curse, and she was afraid for her little girl.

After Angel met Donnie Price, she seemed to settle down for a little while. She started to look less like Wednesday Addams and more like a corn-fed country girl. Even her grades improved. When she begged to go to her Senior Prom, Louise pushed her reservations aside and allowed it.

Determined not to do as her critical mother had done, she never even said a word when Angel chose a deeply cut blood red dress with the entire back out of it. Louise was just happy her little girl had found peace. Angel and Donnie went off to prom together, smiling and waving as Louise made them pose for a picture. It was one of her best memories of Angel, but it was bittersweet.

Not long after that, Angel and Donnie discovered hard drugs. They fell for them hard and fast. Just weeks short of graduation, Angel dropped out and shacked up with Donnie in one of his daddy's trailers over in Conway. The next time Louise saw her she was haggard and high, skinny almost to the point of no return—and six months pregnant. She appeared at Louise's front door sobbing, with a paper bag full of her clothes hanging by her side. Louise put her arms around her and silently led her back home. She took her into the kitchen and made her a fried bologna sandwich and a glass of milk.

It was a new beginning for both of them.

They fixed up a nursery in Angel's old room. Angel got herself a job checking groceries at the local Piggly Wiggly. One day, she told Louise she had taken out a $50,000 life insurance policy on herself and put it in her mother's name. "For my little girl," she said. "I want to make sure she's taken care of." Louise put her arms around her daughter. "She will be," she said. "By you and me! She'll have the bestest Mommy and Mommaw ever!" Angel reached out and patted her hand.

The baby was born and placed in isolation, but Angel never moved again. Even though she had gotten clean and sober during her last trimester, all the hard drug use had taken its toll. She left the world much more quietly than she had entered it 18 years earlier. By the time Louise left the hospital with the tiny baby girl, she had a nice insurance check and a broken heart. She named the baby Misty Dawn Stiltner. She thought it had a nice positive ring to it, for a new beginning.

On the way home, her old Ford gave up the ghost. She had it towed to the nearest dealership, and looked around for a new vehicle to take its place. That's when she saw the rainbow. It had been drizzling all morning, and when the sun cleared the clouds this big beautiful rainbow filled the sky. Instead of a pot of gold, at the end of it sat a used beige Honda Civic. It was perfect. Her new ride. She bought it on the spot, and paid cash.

It wasn't until years later that Rainbow got her nickname. It was Misty Dawn who gave it to her. She was about five years old and toddling around. By this time, she had as her constant companion her favorite doll, the one with brightly-colored orange hair and a rainbow outfit. Louise had found it at a yard sale, and Misty never let it out of her sight. Suddenly, she got a brilliant idea—and like most five-year-olds, just went with it.

It suddenly occurred to Louise that Misty had been far too quiet, for way too long. When Louise came outside to check on her she saw the reason why. The Civic was covered in bright stripes of paint—red, yellow, sea green, pale blue, lavender—as far up as a five-year-old could reach! Misty just looked up and smiled, still holding the paint brush in her hand. She said, "Wook, Mommaw! Wainbow Bwite!" She had used up all the little jars of spare paint from where Louise had painted the bedrooms and rear deck.

Louise couldn't help it. Mad as she was, she started to laugh. She laughed until she knew she had to pee right *now*, so she *ran* to the bathroom. Then she came out and laughed some more. Misty laughed too, and threw on even more paint.

Louise had to admit, it did improve the looks of the car. Over the years, it had developed a few scrapes and bruises. The beige paint had faded in the sun, and that time she had to get the rear quarter panel replaced all they had was a pale blue one. She had planned to get it repainted, but had never gotten around to it. She got out more cans of paint and even some spray cans, and the two of them went to town! On that day, Rainbow

Bright was born. Louise even crocheted an afghan in rainbow stripes to match the car. It took them everywhere, from church meetings, to the drive-in to see Disney princess movies, and much later, when Misty had outgrown them, to see a revival of *Gone with the Wind* and the *Twilight* saga. The three of them were a private club: she, Misty and Rainbow.

Well, not so much lately; it seemed to Louise that Misty had outgrown both her and Rainbow Bright. "Why don't you get that ole heap painted?" she now scoffed. Louise looked at the faded stripes with new and more critical eyes. She just couldn't bring herself to do it. But today everything would be like old times, because today she was taking Misty prom dress shopping. She'd saved a little money for extras: matching pumps or a cute little evening bag. She knew Misty's favorite color was shell pink. She had put all thoughts of the curse into the darkest corner of her mind, and left them there.

"Where should we go first?" Louise asked. "I saw some awful pretty things over at LeAnne's Formals."

Misty took a deep breath. Then she said, "Mommaw, I won't need a dress."

"Why not? Aren't you still going with Christopher?"

"Yeah, sure. But we're going on his motorcycle, so we're just gonna wear our leathers. And our helmets, of course. I won't even need to really get my hair done, 'cause it'll just get squished up with the helmet. I'll just wash it and blow it dry. I have some wildflowers I can weave in once we get there."

On prom night, a nervous Louise watched as the two of them rode off into the night, pale pink corsage and boutonnière flapping in the spring breeze. They had dutifully posed for her to take pictures, standing beside the motorcycle. Louise took Misty aside to briefly whisper, "Now if anything goes on that you don't like or approve of, just call me." Misty hugged her and said, "Have a little faith in me, Mommaw. I can take care of myself!" But she said it with more love than impatience.

As they roared away, Louise thought about how they were planning to stay up all night, as was the new tradition with prom goers. They would attend the dance, then go to a hotel to stay overnight, where there would be games and activities for the entire junior and senior class, finishing off with a buffet breakfast. She realized with a smile that even some of the teens who attended her mother's old church were doing this. How times did change!

She had had a strict curfew, and had tried to impose one on Angel—and look where both of them had ended up. Hoping for the best, she went inside. She read until ten o'clock and then drew the shades. It looked like rain. She fell asleep with the late movie droning softly in the background.

At 1:23 AM, she was awakened by her cell phone blaring out Misty's ringtone. She grabbed for the phone and was met with loud sobbing. "Mommaw! I need you to come *now*! We've had a terrible accident." Outside, it kept thundering and rain poured down. She saw lightning flash across the sky.

"Where are you, Honey? Are you and Christopher OK?"

"We're on Black Star Road. We're both OK; just a little banged up. The motorcycle...it's wrecked pretty good. We got hit by a car as we were leaving the hotel."

"I'm calling the police right now."

"They're already here. So is the Rescue Squad. But I need *you*, Mommaw."

"I'm on my way, Honey. I'll be right there!"

Trembling, she hung up, threw on her clothes, and fished Rainbow's keys out of her jeans pocket. She drove like mad out to toward the hotel until she saw all the flashing lights and a gathering crowd.

Two kids were already loaded into one ambulance. Another was pulling up to get the rest. The car looked like it had been hit by a missile. The motorcycle was a hunk of twisted metal and broken glass. Misty and Christopher were huddled together. Except for some cuts and scrapes, they looked all right. Louise breathed a sigh of relief. Gingerly they walked over to her, with Christopher leading Misty by the hand.

"I'm so sorry, Miz Stiltner. We shouldn't have left the hotel. But I was just trying to look out for Misty. You see, it was getting a little rowdy, and some of the kids were drinking and carrying on. I just didn't want her to be around anything like that, so we decided to just leave. I was taking her home, but then it started raining pretty hard. And then that car was heading straight for us. I just told her to hang on to me, and we both jumped off as fast as we could!" Misty nodded.

"Thank the Good Lord we had our leathers on. It probably saved us. But it was strange; it was like we were sort of floating on the air, there for a minute. When we landed, we both skidded over to the side of the road—just like we'd been thrown or something. It was a miracle!"

She watched as Christopher helped Misty into the passenger side of the car. "Would you like a ride home?" she asked.

"No, I'm good." He pointed to a new black Mercedes that was just pulling up to the scene. "That's Mom and Dad coming right now. We'll finish talking to the police. Tell Midi I'll call her in the morning. I sure hope Dad won't be too mad at me!"

Louise put a hand on his arm. "You did good tonight. Your daddy will be proud of you. And he will just be happy you are okay." She watched the tall young man as he walked away.

As she got in the car, she noticed Misty was shivering. She turned on the heater and pulled the old rainbow ripple-stitch afghan from the back seat, tucking it around her Misty's shoulders. She held her granddaughter until she felt her relax in her arms.

"Mommaw," Misty said, "when I saw you and Rainbow pull up, I felt so warm inside. I knew everything would be okay." She turned and curled further into the seat. "Promise me something: Promise me you won't ever paint Rainbow Bright. She's perfect just the way she is."

Louise couldn't help smiling. "I promise," she said. As she drove along Misty's breathing became smooth and even, and Louise knew she was sleep. She patted the steering wheel lovingly. Then she looked up and prayed a silent prayer. "We did it, my Angel," she said. "I knew you were looking out for her! We finally broke our prom curse. From now on, the Stiltner women are gonna be all right!"

The End

Sallie Borden's Quilt

Betty Kossick

The rain dancing on the tin roof sounds good to Judie. The tap-a-tap-tap arouses her, as she rubs her eyes awake. She lies on her bed with the quilt pulled up to her chin for a long while before she ventures beyond the covers. This morning holds a slight chill, but she knows that the heat will soon press in, because July in Georgia usually simmers. She delights in waking up every morning in the old home built by her husband's great-grandfather. Her fingers trace across the lace rose trim that her grandma added to the quilt she'd made before there was a Judie. Her thought tumbles out, *I miss Grandma.*

Judie's grandma, Sallie Borden, made the quilt for Judie's parents—her son Brady and his wife Ellie—as a wedding gift. Ellie thanked her mother-in-law often for the quilt fashioned with a dove, holding a B-shaped wreath of roses in its beak at the quilt's center, as if the dove were flying over a valley scene. Though Sallie's quilts were sought after, especially the one-of-a-kind quilts she crafted, and she held a reputation as a top-notch Georgian quilt-maker, she never designed another quilt quite like this one. She enjoyed naming each of her unique quilt designs. "Peace in the Valley" seemed the perfect name for this work of art.

Brady and Ellie were sleeping under the quilt when Ellie went into labor. Grandma told Judie many times that it made her feel that she had a special part in her birth, though Judie's twin Trudie was stillborn. Yet Judie often wondered, *Why, me, Lord?*

Judie vowed early in life that if that if she ever birthed a girl-child that she'd name her Trudie. She never felt complete without her twin. She told Grandma, "It's like a part of me isn't."

When Judie married Chester Brown, the quilt became theirs. Grandma died before Judie and Chester's wedding, so Grandma never knew that her quilt became a wedding gift for a second time; it would have pleased her. Ellie insisted that it belong to Judie and Chester, as a memorial to her mother-in-law. "Of course," Ellie noted, "It doesn't hurt that Judie's marryin' a man named Brown, so the embroidered B is fittin'."

This morning, Judie pats her swelling belly thinking, *it matters not if you're a boy or girl. I love you.* Chester had assured Judie many times that he felt the same.

The rain gains momentum, along with stirring wind. Chester awakes. Judie rolls over, hoping for their usual hug before arising. He kisses her on her forehead and places his large carpenter's hand tenderly on her belly. "Well, whatever the baby is, it's a growin'. Not long, my darlin'...six weeks, or so?" He felt the baby move. "Wow! That's some kick! If it's a boy, maybe he'll go to Georgia Tech and play football. Or maybe it's a girl, and she'll be a cheerleader for the team!" Chester laughs. "I'm glad that we haven't done the ultrasound. I'd rather not know until the birth if it's a he or a she."

Judie sits up and stretches. She pushes her auburn hair back from her hazel eyes, and runs her fingers along the cradle that Chester made for their baby. Chester sat the cradle alongside their bed the day he finished it. "This makes me mighty proud to be a carpenter," he told Judie. She reaches for her chenille robe, lying on the bedside chair. As she belts the robe, she feels a strong pain in her back. "Oh, Chester, my back just grabbed me something fierce."

"You okay, Hon?" he frowns. His brown eyes look troubled.

"It's a mean backache," she sighs. Standing upright, bracing her back with both hands, she tries to ease the discomfort. Then, a nauseating pain alerts her that it's time. "Chester, hurry outta that bed. I think the baby's comin'!"

"It isn't time," Chester calls to her, as he hurries into his trousers.

"But it is, Chester. We gotta' hurry! Oh, honey, the water's just broke."

...The next morning...

Brady Borden looks at his granddaughter through the window in the maternity ward, with his arm around Ellie. "Doesn't seem any time since we did this window peekin' for Judie, does it? Remember that thatch of brown-reddish hair she had right off? A beauty then, and still is."

Ellie bites her lower lip, "God's given us a second chance. It looks like He's blessed us with a healthy Trudie this time: our granddaughter Trudie. She's a tiny thing, comin' so early and all, but Doc tells Judie that she'll be just fine, even if she does have to spend a bit of time in an incubator. Preemies make it these days. But she is a wee one at four pounds, ten ounces."

"Sure wish my momma coulda' seen this one. She'd be mighty proud," Brady sighs.

Hand in hand, Ellie and Brady walk back to Judie's room. Doc Evans is talking with Judie and Chester when they walk in.

"Hello, Doc," Brady extends his hand. "Well, what do you think of your granddaughter, Brady Borden?" Doc asks.

"I just told Ellie, she's somethin' else."

"Mom, Dad," Judie interrupts, "Doc thinks that because Trudie is so small that she needs to stay here in the hospital for few days. He says that her lungs are strugglin' a bit. He calls it respiratory distress syndrome, and with an immature immune system we shouldn't take any chances."

"This isn't what we expected," Chester says, as he squeezes Judie's hand.

"I'd say that's wisdom," Brady nods to Doc.

Ellie turns a worried look at Doc, but quickly turns to Judie with a smile. She doesn't want to worry her daughter. She's not forgotten all those years ago, when Judie and her twin were born. Ellie's heart still feels the wound.

...Two days later...

Morning breaks with brilliant sunshine. But for Judie the day seems dismal; her tears flow by the time Chester arrives at her room to take her home. She buries her face in his jacket and sobs, "How can I leave her, Chester?"

Pulling her close to him, Chester comforts his wife. "Well, Hon, we only live ten miles out of town, you'll be comin' back to nurse her, and savin' milk for her if you can't be here every nursing. In the meantime, you need to get some tight sleepin' in."

"I know... I know, Chester. Let's take one more peek at Trudie before we take off."

The quiet hum of the hospital nursery and the kind eyes of the nurses provide assurance to Judie and Chester as they watch Trudie squirming in her incubator bassinette. "She looks absolutely beautiful, even when she's wigglin'," Judie insists. Chester laughs, "The bitsy's already wiggled her way into my heart, that's for sure."

"Chester, we have a lot to thank the Lord for, don't we?"

"Yes, Hon. Why don't we thank Him right now, before we leave?" He grasps her hands and prays, "Dear God, you've been mighty good to us. We thank you a heap, and we promise to rear this princess you gave us to love You."

...Three weeks later...

"Oh, Chester, I'm so glad that you're takin' some vacation time to be with Trudie and me for a few days. The three of us need this bondin' time, now that she's home."

"Hon, I know that the medical bills are far more than expected, with the extra care Trudie required, and $12,000 is a heap of money, but bein' together like this is important. I'll get some side work. We'll figure it out," Chester said. He opened the *Blue Ridge Gazette* while finishing off breakfast with a cup of warm, sweet sassafras tea.

When he lays down the newspaper, Judie picks it up. Flipping through it, she spies a large half-page ad. The words catch her attention.

Quilts of Original Design Contest, Grand Prize $10,000, First and Second prizes of $5,000 and $2,500. Each quilt must be titled. The quilters whose quilts are not chosen as winners can sell their quilts at the show. Entries: September 1. Winners announced: October 15.

Grandma's quilt! The contest rules seem simple enough, she muses. She reads on.

The grand winner's quilt design will become temporary property of the Southern Belle Quilt Museum in Tuckerton for a year, then be used as a tour quilt to be taken across the United States for prestigious quilt shows for another year.

Judie tosses the thought in her mind: *It's only two years.* And it would be an honor for Sallie Borden's memory, for her design to be honored by other quilters. Judie knew what she must do. Her mind raced. *This is the answer to payin' our medical debt! I won't tell Chester, I'll just enter it and surprise him. I know Grandma's quilt is not new, but it's in top-notch condition, and it's one-of-a-kind.*

Trudie's whimpering calls for Judie's attention. Chester's already holding her out to her mother. "Breakfast time for baby, too," he grins. As she cuddles Trudie close for nursing, she's thinking of the possibility of Grandma's quilt winning. *Ah,* she thinks again, *I take the quilt off the bed for summer anyhow, so Chester won't even realize anythin's different.*

...Another two weeks pass...

"Chester, I haven't driven the car except to the hospital since Trudie's birth. I think it's time I get rollin' again. Trudie's up to gettin' out now. Sometime this week, I'd like to do that."

"That's a good idea, wife of mine. She made a big hit at church this week, didn't she?"

Judie smiles. "Wasn't that sweet, about Gail and Brad Braddock sayin' since their Sam is only a year older than Trudie, that we might think about promisin' her to him? It would be mighty nifty of her to grow up and marry the son of good friends."

"Yep, and with the name of Braddock, we could pass on Grandma's quilt to them," Chester suggested. "That is, if you'd be willin' part with it."

"Sure, like a tradition," Judie agrees, feeling a twinge of guilt for not telling Chester about the quilt contest. *I just don't want him to get his hopes up if Grandma's design doesn't win. I know he's worried about payin' the medical bills. Georgia's got a bunch of excellent quilt makers, yet I know that Grandma was one of its finest.*

...The next day...

As soon as Chester leaves for work, Judie launders Grandma's quilt. Like her mother, she never hung the quilt outside to dry for fear of sun-fading. Smart caution helped preserve Grandma's quilt. *When it dries, I'll have Chester put it away and he'll think that's where it is.*

A week later, Judie's off to Tuckerton, where the entries are to be sub-mitted. As she stands in line, she spies Leah Grayling three rows ahead, holding a quilt to submit. Leah had moved to Roseville, and Judie hadn't seen her for a few years. She remembered Leah took quilting lessons from Grandma—and that Grandma always bragged on Leah: "That young girl's got a gift, with her nimble fingers and good stitchin.' And she's mighty good with designs, too." *I'm sure her quilt will give Grandma's good competition. I won't call out to her now. When I'm done, I'll go greet her.*

She fills out the entry forms and hands over the quilt to Ruth Hasty, the registrar, with a nudge of trepidation. *What if somethin' happens to it?* When she finishes, she looks to see if Leah is still in the room. *Yes, there she is!*

"Hello, Leah! Long time, no see."

"Judie! I wondered if your family might submit a Sallie Borden quilt. But I figured I might as well try."

"Grandma would be so happy that you did, Leah. She was always a braggin' on your stitchin' gift."

"So, Judie, you're a momma now?"

"This is Trudie, Leah. We feel so blessed to have her. It's good to see you, Leah, even if we are competin.' Let's hope we both place."

"Wouldn't that be nice? I really wanted to do this to honor your grannie's memory. I'd not be a quilter, except for her teachin' me. But I am also hopin' to win one of the cash prizes, because I want to go back to college and study to be an elementary school teacher. My Garland is six years old now, and it's time I did what I told your granny I planned to do."

"I guess we're both in need of money," Trudie sympathizes. "We've got big bills to pay because Trudie came early, needin' special doctorin' and attention."

"Let's sit together at the quilt festival, when the judgin' is held, okay?' Leah asks. "It sure is good seein' you, Trudie."

...Three weeks later...

Chester pushes his chair back from his mother-in-law's kitchen table. "That is some cookin' you did, Mama Borden."

"Yum, Mom," Judies adds. "Thanks for havin' us for supper. Sorry that Daddy had to work overtime."

"I'll warm up a plate for him as soon as he steps in the house," Ellie assures her daughter.

With the slam of the back door, Chester, Judie, and Ellie all shout in unison, "He's home!"

"Mighty good smellin' vittles," Brady says, then kisses his wife.

"We were just gettin' ready for some blackberry cobbler, but you eat your dinner first," Ellie insists.

Judie checks on sleeping Trudie as Brady digs into his food. After a couple of mouthfuls, he asks, "Did y'all hear about the big fire in Tuckerton? I was listen' to the news on the truck radio on my way home. If Mama were alive, she'd be mighty sad about the Southern Belle Quilt Museum a-blazin' down."

"*No!* Daddy, please, *no!* It can't be!" Judie cries out.

Chester rushes to Judie. "Hon, what's ailin' you? Why are you so upset?"

"Please, I've got to get to Tuckerton immediately. Grandma's quilt is there: at the museum. I entered it for a big contest, hopin' to win some of the prize money to pay Trudie's bills. And Leah Chapman, Grandma's prize student, also entered a quilt. This is devastatin'."

Ellie places Brady's dinner in the refrigerator and they all pile into Brady's car together. Ellie holds baby Trudie, and Chester tries to comfort Judie as Brady drives. It's a short drive, but it seems like an eternity—and the smell of billowing smoke makes Judie feel nauseous. "Grandma's quilt didn't deserve this kind of an endin'."

The car turns onto Peachtree Courtyard Boulevard. The police barrier stops them. Judie jumps out, asking, "Is everythin' burned?"

She hears, "Ma'am, it's not likely anythin' in that inferno could be saved."

"*Judie!*" She turns to see Leah. And with her is Ruth Hasty, the registrar for the quilts. "Judie, praise God, the quilts... They aren't burned! Miss Hasty says all the entries were stored in a vault at the Grey Mountain Bank and Trust. But look, the museum is ashes."

Judie, still sobbing, rushes past Leah and up to Miss Hasty. "Thank, you, thank you," She cries, then darts back to Leah.

Miss Hasty comes over to Leah and Judie and encircles them both in a hug. "Yes, it must be the Lord's hand in savin' the entries, because the judgin' committee just came up with the idea of the vault storage yesterday. This all came about because of a recent neighborhood break-in. There are two hundred twenty-seven entries, and I'd consider them all priceless, with amazin' designs and needlework. One of the quilt patrons is the president of the bank. He suggested it, and arranged for some of the bank employees to volunteer their time to transport the quilts to the vaults. It's a shame to lose the museum, but a blessing that it was closed—with no one inside. Good thing we're insured."

Through all the commotion, baby Trudie sleeps well. "I hope you aren't upset with me, Chester, for not tellin' you my plan to try to get us some money for the bills. It doesn't really matter if Grandma's quilt wins or not now, I'm just glad it was rescued—and all the others, too."

"Hon," Chester smiles, "the idea is a great one. And I must admit, it is a good idea to try. But from what the registrar said, it sounds like it will be stiff competition. The judges will have a job decidin', won't they?"

"Momma, final judgin' is in three weeks, can you come with me?"

"Wouldn't miss it!" Ellie smiles.

...Three weeks later...

"Chester, today's the quilt judging. I'm really gettin' nervous about it. The winnin's important, but it isn't important, you know what I mean? After the fire, it just nice to know that no one—and no quilt— was hurt."

"If we win, we win; if we don't, we don't. My bid is in to build the cabinetry for the new Tucker Golf Course Clubhouse. If I get it, that will help a lot," Chester reminds Judie, as he kisses her cheek on his way out the door. "Call me as soon as you know anything. Love you."

"Me too!" Judie says, as she stretches up for another kiss.

Chester pulls out of the driveway just as Ellie is pulling in. They wave at each other, and Ellie hurries out of the car to help Judie with Trudie.

"Ready for the big day, Honey?"

"As ready as I'll ever be, Momma."

As they pull onto the grounds of the Evergreen Country Club, Judie sighs. "Imagine how excited Grandma would be if she were here."

"*Juuudie!* I've saved seats for us." Judie recognizes Leah calling.

Judie thrusts her right index finger forward. "I see Miss Hasty sittin' in the front row."

A tall, slender, neatly-bearded man walks up to the microphone. "Travis Simms is my name. I'm honored to serve as the master of ceremonies here today. I'm a quilter just like many of you. My grandmother headed this event for many years. She's also the one who taught me to quilt. I'm honored to serve today as she did.

"I know we're all grateful that these quilts are able to be displayed today. They all came so close to being a part of that terrible fire three weeks ago.

We'll miss that old museum terribly, yet we have our mighty good memories of it. Only ashes now lie where the Southern Belle Quilt Museum stood for sixty-seven years. We've all shed tears over this turn of events. However, a phoenix will rise out of those ashes! Land has been donated by a patron in Coopersville, Imogene Cooper, and construction will begin in short order."

When the applause stops, Travis continues. "All of you are anxious to know who the winners are today. So am I, so let's get on with the show. We'll begin with quilt judge Carrie Lynn Rochester, who will announce the winning quilts."

"As you all know," Carrie Lynn says, "there are three major cash prizes in this contest: three, out of two hundred twenty-seven wonderful quilts. It was hard work for the seven judges to decide on the winners, yet our consensus was mutual. However, we have a surprise; there were so many outstanding designs that we added a bonus to this contest, thanks to one of the museum's patrons: three honorable mention cash prizes, of $1,000 each." Carrie Lynn is interrupted by the surprised audience. As the clapping stops, she smiles. "Please come forward as I call each name and quilt title. Third honorable mention, 'Meadow' by Cora Beth Summers; second honorable mention, 'Cats at Play' by Tom Barrow; first honorable mention, 'Nightscape' by Bobbie Sue Parks." Applause resounds with each announcement.

"Remember, folks, after the announcements are finished for all the winners, all entrants are invited to stand or sit by their work, and those quilters whose quilts haven't won cash prizes are allowed to sell their quilts at that time.

"Now—the second-place winner, of $2,500, is 'Mountain View,' by Leah Grayling." Leah gasps as she hears the quilt title.

Judie beams at Leah. "My Grandma would be mighty proud of you, Leah."

"First place winner is 'Quiet Streams,' by Caroline Mattson." A young woman wheels forward in a motorized wheelchair to receive her prize of $5,000.

"OK, folks, we've all been waiting for the grand prize. And here it is: The winner asked that if her entry wins, the winner be announced as the late Sallie Borden. *Am I hearin' right?* Judie thinks. *I asked that.* Ellie reaches for her daughter's hand and squeezes it. "Sallie designed and made 'Peace in the Valley,' but Judie Brown, her granddaughter, entered the inherited original design quilt. Congratulations, Judie; Sallie just won just won the grand prize of $10,000."

With applause sounding in her ears, Judie walks forward to join the other winners. Leah hugs her tightly. "Now it's my turn, Judie. Your Grandma would be mighty proud." Judie looks out at the room full of quilters, who are still applauding, then looks up and whispers, "A mighty thank you, Lord."

The End

The Cupboard

Susanna Connelly Holstein

Sweat ran down the back of her neck as Ella stretched on tiptoes to spread flour paste inside the cupboard. It wasn't yet full daylight, but she had grabbed a few minutes before starting breakfast to start putting paper on the rough wood shelves. Jim would be down any minute so she worked quickly, listening for his footsteps on the stairs that led up to their bedroom. She grabbed the roll of wallpaper and cut a strip, pushing it carefully into place.

August was a month of hard work on the farm. The threshers would be coming soon, with their big machine to harvest the wheat. The corn was ripening and the hay would soon be ready for another cutting. Tomatoes, beans, corn, squash, and cucumbers filled her days with steamy heat in the kitchen as she put up jar after jar of colorful produce for the coming winter. The cabinet was not a necessary chore and she knew it, but she yearned for a pretty place to put the dishes left to her by her grandmother;

now she had it. All it needed was a little pretty paper to brighten up the dark interior.

A door closed upstairs, and Ella flew to the stove. She was pouring boiling water over coffee grounds as Jim stomped downstairs. Ella pulled bacon, biscuits, and gravy from the warming oven, put the bowls on the table, and began cracking eggs into a heated cast iron skillet.

"Morning, Sunshine." Jim gave her a quick peck on the cheek and grabbed a mug. Ella smiled at her tall husband. Even though his hair was beginning to thin on top and there were lines beginning to etch the corners of his eyes, he still made her heart give a little leap whenever he smiled at her.

The aroma of strong coffee filled the room. Jim sighed and took a long sip as Ella lifted her cup and saucer from a shelf and poured her tea from a china teapot. She had never acquired a taste for the bitterness of coffee, preferring tea with milk and sugar to start her day.

"The threshers are over at Nelson's this morning," Jim said. "I'm going over to give them a hand after I get my chores done. They'll be here to help us later, when the machine comes to our place. Do you want to go along and visit with Mary?"

Ella shook her head. "I'd like to, but I really can't. I have two bushels of tomatoes in the cellar waiting on me this morning, and I really want to finish this cupboard today and get it all put in place." She glanced at the cupboard. The wallpaper really was going to look good.

Jim laughed. "You and that cabinet. I can't see the use of it; really, I can't. You would have been better off to keep those berries for yourself. I know Old Man Smithson didn't need that cabinet. He just made himself a mighty fine deal, getting all those blackberries. Why, you could have made us a dozen pies with them!" He winked at her.

"You think only of your stomach, mister. We have plenty of berries in the cellar already! I know you think its woman's foolishness, but I have wanted a place to put Grandma's china for ever so long. What good is it to keep it stored away in crates in the attic?"

"What good is china anyway, Honey? These old plates are good enough for me." Jim thunked his fork on the heavy brown plate in front of him.

"But don't overdo it today. The threshers will be here this week, and you'll have a lot of cooking to do. Those fellas eat a powerful lot of food, you know. Will you be up to it, in your condition?" He glanced at her softly rounded belly.

"I'll be ready. The ladies from church are coming over to help, and they'll be bringing plenty of food with them, thank goodness. Oh, you can take these two peach pies over to Mary today when you go. She'll be pleased to get them, I know."

Jim finished eating and pushed back from the table. "All right, then." He pulled her to him and gave her a gentle hug and a soft peck on the cheek. She smiled and snuggled into his firm chest for a moment before pulling away.

"Go on, mister! Enough foolishness! We've both got plenty to do today!"

Jim laughed, picked up his hat, and walked out the door. Ella watched him walk to the barn and listened to him calling the horses. It was going to be a hot day, that was certain. Heat shimmered on the dusty road already. She went back inside to clear away the dishes. A little while later, Jim's shout called her to the porch. She carried the pies out and waved goodbye as the wagon jounced up the road and out of sight.

While dishwater heated on the wood cookstove, she worked on papering the inside of her new cupboard. *Well, not new,* she thought, *but new to me. I wonder how long it's been around, and where Mr. Smithson got it?* He'd been a bachelor all his life, so perhaps it had belonged to his mother. He was a sly one, that old man. He'd seen her walking home with her buckets of berries last week, and had offered to trade the cupboard for the berries.

"I don't need the thing, I sure don't. It's just in my way. I remember how you admired it once, so I would be glad to swap you for those fine berries."

Ella didn't hesitate. "It's a deal, Mr. Smithson!" she'd said, laughing. He brought the cupboard over that same evening, staying for supper and some cobbler out on the cool porch afterwards. Jim was puzzled, but he said after all, they were her berries—and if she wanted to trade her hard work for some old cabinet, who was he to argue?

She sat on the porch in her wicker rocker years later, wrinkled hands folded neatly in her lap and her gray hair pulled back in a bun. Her tired blue eyes swept the scene in front of her. People bustled in and out, talking in quiet voices, looking at the furniture, dishes, tools, and farm equipment spread out on the lawn for the auction to be held that day. The old cupboard was under the maple tree, its well-worn finish dull in the harsh light of day. Ella remembered how pretty it had been filled with white china, and how proud she had been of this showpiece in her kitchen.

Over the years, the china had been broken, piece by piece. As the decades passed the delicate English pieces were replaced, first with pink and green Depression glass, later with Homer Laughlin's cheaper lines of dinnerware, and finally with plastic Melamine. Thin china cups gave way to Fire King mugs. Children—five of them—were born, grew up, and eventually moved on to homes of their own. The flour paste had dried out over the years, and Ella had used thumbtacks to hold the paper in place. Now the faded design was barely discernible, and the paper hung loose here and there. She hadn't had the energy or the desire to fix it after Jim got sick. After he died, she had tried to keep the farm going, but it was too much for her. She had finally agreed that it was time to sell out and move in with her oldest son and his family.

She sighed. It was going to take some getting used to, being with other people and in another woman's home. Hardest of all was letting go of the things she had loved all these years, especially that cupboard. Her son had offered to bring it over to his place when she moved, but Ella knew there was no place for it—and truth be told, it did look pretty bad. *It hasn't fared any better than I have*, Ella thought. The years had worn them both down, but they were good years; she had been blessed. She had to remember that. At least she had family willing to take her in, instead of whisking her off to some nursing home.

A young woman wandered over to the old cupboard. Ella watched as the woman pulled open the doors and lifted the peeling paper.

"Cathy, are you seriously looking at that?" A man, looking to be in his late twenties, sauntered over and put his arm around the young woman. She looked up at him and smiled.

"Oh yeah! Look at this thing! See how someone whittled a piece to keep the doors closed? And some lady put this paper in here to make it pretty, but it's in bad shape. She tried to keep it in place with thumbtacks when it came loose. It's rough for sure, but I can fix it up, David, I know I can."

The man shrugged. "Suit yourself. Are you going to bid on it? I can't see what we need it for, but if you want it, go ahead."

"I want it. You wait 'til you see how pretty it is with my grandmother's china in it."

The End

The News

Lori C. Byington

On a crisp fall day, when the leaves are at their zenith in colors of amber, orange, red and saffron, Myrtle Counts walks numbly from her '69 Packard to the porch of the house she and husband of thirty years, Tal (short for Talmadge) lovingly call home. *The porch stoop is in need of a coat of white paint*, Myrtle thinks to herself. *The paint can wait until spring, though. A rough winter is predicted, so there's no need to do a job that will have to be done again in a few months.* As she gathers her baby-blue knit scarf close, and her courage closer, Myrtle walks firmly to the front stoop. She pauses to take a deep breath. As she looks to the exceptionally blue fall sky, Myrtle exhales. The familiar ghosts of another time escape her pursed, pale lips. Through the front window, she sees her husband waiting impatiently at the worn oak kitchen table. Myrtle can see he has been wringing a damask blue and white napkin to bits while he waited. After putting her scarf and navy wool coat on the rack at the front door, she looks at her husband. His eyes are questioning and apprehensive. Myrtle's eyes meet his questioning gaze, and her tears almost rush out—but not yet.

Tal rushes to Myrtle as he declares, "Sorry I couldn't accompany you. Had a sick cow that wasn't nursin', an' the chickens needed fed, an' I had to get the eggs, an'... Tal lets out a rattling, wet breath. Myrtle can tell he's been crying, though he would never admit to such.

Myrtle interrupts suddenly and a bit harshly. "It's OK, love. I know."

As Myrtle walks into the kitchen to get a china cup to pour some of the tea she had made earlier, Tal pulls out a chair beside him at the table as suggestion for Myrtle to "light" somewhere.

"I'll sit directly," Myrtle promises and fakes a slightly crooked smile.

Her soft blue eyes meet his gray-green ones, and he knows. As if they had telepathy between one another, he knows the doctor's news. Tal's heart falls to his feet and a sweat like none he has ever had before in his life erupts from his lined, tanned forehead. As his hands tremble, Tal tries to pick up his half-empty coffee cup. Body and mind do not work together though; the blue and cream-colored Poppyfield cup from their wedding trousseau falls silently to the newly swept floor. The cup drifts downward, in an achingly slow motion only a well-oiled oak plank can stop. The heirloom shatters, and as the cup disintegrates so do plans for the immediate future. Myrtle steps over to help Pa with the cup. As she reaches for a sliver of the cup's remains, Pa reaches too. Their hands touch, then quickly clasp. As Myrtle and Pa's eyes meet, pent up tears begin to flow like rolling waves during a hurricane. Slowly, almost floating, Myrtle and Tal stand up and hug. Gripping each other as if they had already lost one another, sobs of disbelief, terror, confusion and loss of faith wrack their still strong bodies. Thoughts flood both of their minds: *What happened? From where did this disease sneak, silently, angrily, and with no purpose? Why us?* Grasping and clinging to one another, Myrtle and Tal had not cleaved so hard since the last time they had "loved." When had that been? Time and life's callings got in the way. Now, time is of the essence.

Myrtle and Tal gather their emotions, and themselves, enough to pull each other up from the floor. Tal wipes his reddened eyes and asks, "What did the doctor say? Tell me all."

Tal holds her arm, and Myrtle takes the Carolina oak- spindled chair Tal had pulled out for her a few minutes before. She wipes her eyes and face with the wrinkled napkin Tal used earlier, and lets out a long, slow breath.

"Whew! Well, Doctor Crockett says I have something called stage two invasive ductal carcinoma, but I don't know much what he means. I guess I have the cancer, Tal," Myrtle admits with tears in her sky-blue eyes. "He says I can have the whole mess removed with surgery, easy as pie, an' then I'll have to have that drug that makes my hair fall out, and then probably something called radiation. That part sounds like something from Oak Ridge or Oppenheimer's bomb! It all scares me to pieces, really."

Myrtle laughs a little when she tells Tal, but her insides aren't laughing at all. She was bone scared. Tal puts his arm around her and gently lays her head in the crook of his strong shoulder. He prays she won't feel him shaking. Silently, Tal wishes he had gone with Myrtle to the doctor to be her anchor, but he didn't imagine her news would be so devastating.

"There, there," he says quietly. "We'll do this together, like every other mess we've had to clamber out of. I guess the next thing we need to do is find out when and where the doctor wants to do everything. The nearest teachin' hospital is in Winston-Salem. I wonder if the doc will send you there. 'Twould only be a two-hour drive from Bristol. Not far, really, as the crow flies."

Myrtle sniffs and wipes her youthful face again. She sits up from Tal's shoulder, pushes her curly, golden blond hair back from her creased brow, and sniffs again. Defiantly, but shaking, she tells Tal, "OK. I guess I need to do this. I need to get this disease out of me so it doesn't spread somewhere else. I have heard tell of others who did not do as the doctors said, and the cancer spread to other body parts. I don't want that to happen. I want this bugger out! Now!"

Tal looks at the love of his life and realizes again some of the reasons he married her. She has spunk and gumption and takes no bull. He takes his work-worn hand and pushes Myrtle's hair back off of her face, then slowly leans over and kisses her gently on her trembling lips. A sigh of release escapes them both, and, suddenly, they know what they have to do.

"I'll call the doctor tomorrow and schedule my surgery. We will get through this damn thing, and be stronger for it," announces Myrtle as she stands up, firmly, from the table. She nervously wipes crumbs from their long-ago break-fast into her hand and walks over to the sink. She turns from Tal to drop the crumbs into the sink, and forces her hands to stop shaking. Myrtle turns back to her husband and looks into his green-gray eyes.

Tal forces a smile and nods his head in response and admittance. He knows he will have the hardest time. Tal thinks, *What if!* This simple question is the only thought that runs through his jostled mind, but he does not let on. He must stay strong for Myrtle's sake. Thoughts of life without her invade his mind, but Tal forces such ideas to the back of his mind. He must focus on taking care of the farm—actually, on finding someone to take care of his farm while he helps Myrtle. He never imagined he would have to worry about the love of his life in such a manner. Tal forces himself to plan ahead while his mind is on the present and Myrtle's future.

Tal coughs to clear his throat and says with confidence, "You do that, Myrtle. Make sure the doc knows I'll be with you all the way. I'll get Charles to take care of things around here when we are gone—no worries there. Mr. White will help out, too. He can make sure the cows get milked and the eggs get used and put up. The turkeys won't be ready for Thanksgiving yet, so I can deal with that a bit later."

Myrtle forces a smile and clears her throat. Then, in a confident voice, she says, "Now Tal, don't you fret none. I am a strong woman, and I won't back down from a fight. I never have given up, and I won't now! Many other incredible women have gone to battle with this disease before me. Doc says I am only one in six or maybe eight women who are given such news, so I must be strong for my 'sisters' who are also in the fight against breast cancer." With the words Myrtle speaks, both she and Tal realize they have been forced into a family to which they do not want to belong. Myrtle's blue eyes meet Tal's gray-green ones, and they realize why they love and have loved one another. Their answer to Myrtle's news is set before them as clear as the crisp, blue-sky day that dawned many hours before.

Tal attempts another weak smile. He opens his arms wide, and Myrtle smiles back. She walks steadily into his welcoming, strong arms, takes a deep breath, and smells the cattle, the hay, and their life. She quietly whispers, "Thank you."

The End

About the Authors

Rebecca Spindler
"High Time: Get a Load of Those Shoes"

Rebecca Williams Spindler is an award-winning screenwriter, novelist, short story writer and instructor of young adult fiction at University of Wisconsin-Madison Continuing Studies. Rebecca co-wrote a middle grade/young adult novel series with her teen daughter, Madelyn, for Little Creek Books. She's a member of the International Screenwriters Association and the Society for Children's Book Writers and Illustrators. Follow her on Facebook at www.facebook.com/fansofspindlerwriting, and visit her website at www.spindlerwriting.com.

Linda Hudson Hoagland
"My Decision" and "A Changed Woman"

Linda Hudson Hoagland has won acclaim for her mystery novels, including the recent *Onward & Upward*, *Missing Sammy*, and *Snooping Can Be Helpful–Sometimes*. She is also the author of several works of nonfiction, a collection of short writings, and a volume of poems. Hoagland has won numerous awards for her work, including first place for the Pearl S. Buck Award for Social Change and the Sherwood Anderson Short Story Contest. Learn more about her at www.lindasbooksandangels.com, or contact her at lhhoagland@gmail.com.

Charlotte H. Deskins
"By the Light of the Moon" and "Rainbow Bright"

Charlotte H. Deskins was born in Welch, West Virginia and grew up in the nearby town of War. Those magical hills and hollows fed her imagination and nurtured her love of words. She and her husband, Tom, now live in Abingdon, surrounded by an enchanted wood filled with birds and wildlife. She wrote "Rainbow Bright" for the *Easter Lilies* collection.

Katie Meade
"Climbing a Ladder with Thorns"

Katie Meade, a graduate from the University of Virginia and Morehead State University, has been writing and keeping journals for decades. Her most recent work is *Just a Good Story*. Other books include *A Man Called Hatchet Jack*, *The Rainbow Ghosts*, and *Chucky the Chocolate Mouse*, which are children's books. *Stories from a Coal Camp: A Place of Yesterday* is among the author's published books for adults. Katie lives in Virginia, with her husband Jack and dog Abby.

Susan Robinson Butler
"Snowflakes"

Susan Butler grew up in Lebanon, Virginia. She lives with her husband and two sons in the Northern Neck of Virginia, where she teaches high school Spanish. When she isn't writing, Susan enjoys baking, walking her dog, and spending time with her family. She is currently working on a middle-grade fantasy fiction series. Susan can be reached at susanrobinsonbutler@gmail.com.

Sharyn Martin
"I Promised" and "Last One to Leave"

Sharyn Martin is a local writer who has been published in the literary journal of UVA/Wise, the *Jimson Weed*. She has also won short story and essay competitions published in *Explorations*, an online art and literary journal of Mountain Empire Community College, as well as winning the adult non-fiction writing contest for the Appalachian Heritage Writers Symposium. She has also won the Lonesome Pine Short Story Contest.

Susan Harmon
"A Kindred Spirit"

Susan Noe Harmon is a native of Harlan, Kentucky. She is the author of the novel *Under the Weeping Willow*, and the memoir *To Hide the Truth*. Other works include short stories in several Appalachian anthologies. Although presently living in Florida, her heart remains in the mountains of Kentucky with its people.

Willie E. Dalton
"Patchwork Hearts"

Willie E. Dalton is a full-time writer and the author of *Three Witches in a Small Town*, as well as winner of the 2015 Jan-Carol Publishing Believe and Achieve award. You can find out more about her and read more of her work at www.threewitchesinasmalltown.wordpress.com.

Betty Kossick
"Sallie Borden's Quilt"

Betty Kossick is a freelance writer. Her career spans 45 years; she has written for newspapers and magazines, complied books, and written three books of her own—she's even written greeting cards. The end of 2016 found her byline in 80 books. She's won awards for her writing, and is frequently in the winners' circle for poetry. Contact Betty at bkwrites4u@hotmail.com.

Susanna Connelly Holstein
"The Cupboard"

Susanna Holstein maintains and writes for her blog, *Storyteller Granny Sue: Stories from the Mountains and Beyond*. Her poetry, nonfiction and fiction works have won numerous awards at the WV Writers Annual Conference. Holstein also writes an online journal, *Granny Sue's News and Reviews*, the poetry blog *Mountain Poet*, and a monthly column for the central West Virginia publication *Two Lane Livin'*. Her work has appeared in two anthologies of stories about Appalachian women, as well as in other print and online journals. When not writing, researching or telling stories, she enjoys gardening, canning, and a country lifestyle on her small farm in Jackson County. Contact her at: susannaholstein@yahoo.com. Visit her on the web at: www.grannysu.blogspot.com, www.grannysue.blogspot.com, www.mountainpoet.wordpress.com, www.twolanelivin.com, www.facebook.com/grannysu.

Lori C. Byington
"The News"

Lori Byington lives in Bristol, TN with her husband, Mark, and son, Lee. She is an assistant professor of English at King University. She loves to teach and write. During the winter, she loves her snow skis, and is known as "Ski Mom" because her son races downhill slalom and giant slalom for Team Beech/Beech Mountain Academy, a snow-skiing team based in Beech Mountain, NC. She loves to cook and bake in her free time.

Jan-Carol
Publishing, Inc

"every story needs a book"

LITTLE CREEK BOOKS
MOUNTAIN GIRL PRESS
EXPRESS EDITIONS
DIGISTYLE
ROSEHEART

JANCAROLPUBLISHING.COM